Crimson Cord

JENIFER JENNINGS

Editor: Jill Monday

Scripture quotations and paraphrases are taken from the Holy Bible, King James Version, Copyright © 1977, 1984, 2001 by Thomas Nelson, Inc.

This book is a work of historical fiction based closely on real people and events recorded in the Holy Bible. Details that cannot be historically verified are purely products of the author's imagination. Any resemblance to actual persons, living or dead, or actual events is purely coincidental.

Peacock Press
3040 Plantation Ridge Drive
Green Cove Springs, FL 32043

To my children.
When the tunnel of life seems too dark,
remember God's glorious light is waiting on the
other side.

A Note of Warning

"By faith the harlot Rahab perished not with them that believed not, when she had received the spies with peace."
-HEBREWS11:31

Dear Reader,

In His infinite wisdom, God made sure Rahab's story made it into His Holy Word.

Rahab was a woman who had wasted most of her life on the pleasures of the flesh. In one moment, she seemed to turn her back on everything she had ever known to accept a God whom she had never met. As a result of this one moment of faith, Rahab is lifted high and her name added to a list of the most faithful people of God anyone could ever write. It just goes to show how tender hearted our God is toward those who follow after Him.

To you, Dear Reader, I write this brief word of warning. The following story is fictional, but it's based on the few details of Rahab from the Biblical account found in the book of Joshua. Since Rahab was a known prostitute living in a culture which openly used the human body in several vial ways, there may be some uncomfortable scenes to face. The real story of

Rahab was far more graphic and unimaginable than anyone could pen. Please don't let any of that stop you from taking in Rahab's entire story. I've tried to be cautious in what I've included in this novel. My goal is for you to see how God loves to step in to direct people who are willing to put their trust in Him.

Rahab traded her empty life of pain for a statement of faith. That choice also brought forth a promise God had made long before Rahab was even born. Rahab's small profession of faith in God opened the floodgates of blessings for the people of Israel. God would send His son Jesus, born from a line which counted the gentile harlot Rahab as one of its direct ancestors. Jesus would come into the world to pay the price of every sin ever committed, including Rahab's. We can be made clean and have our lives transformed if we, like Rahab, come to God with one simple confession, "He is God in heaven above, and in earth beneath." -Joshua 2:11.

~Jenifer Jennings

Chapter 1

"And they served their idols: which were a snare unto them."
-PSALM 106:36

1430 B.C., Jericho

Flames of pain rushed through Rahab. Her arms and legs pleaded to be moved to relieve their stiffness.

She tried to lift her head, but felt a sudden wave of sickness come up from her stomach. Managing to turn her head just in time, she threw up her last meal of stew. Rahab twisted away to avoid staring at the dark puddle which colored the sandy street beside her.

The cool night in Jericho should have provided easier breathing compared to the heat of the day. But Rahab had trouble breathing from the weight pressing down on her chest.

She took a slow, steady breath.

What happened?

A loud crash startled Rahab. Forcing her eyes open as wide as she could make them, she searched for the source of the noise.

No one was around, but she was sure she had heard something.

Rahab noticed movement about a stone's throw away from where she lay.

She opened her mouth to scream, but was surprised at the sound which came gurgling up from her throat. It was low and broken, and reminded Rahab of a wounded animal suffering at the hands of an unskilled hunter. Her lips burned with fire as if she had been wandering in the desert for days without a drop of water.

As Rahab lay there trying to find another way to get the person's attention, the flutter of activity drew closer toward her. A surge of fear rose up her back. Something was wrong and her instinct was viciously trying to warn her of danger.

She strained to move. Agony roared forward like waves crashing on the banks of the Jordan River.

A shape slowly came into focus through the

meager slits through which Rahab now saw her world. Misshapen proportions gave indication the being was not only not human, it wasn't natural.

Rusty skin of peeling layers covered by small spikes of metal formed a slinky animal Rahab could not recall from her memory. It moved with hesitation toward her. All four legs were of slightly differing lengths, but it seemed to favor the back two for walking while the front two scraped the ground. Eyes of red stared at Rahab's as it edged ever closer.

Fighting the increasing pain to hold her eyes open, Rahab searched the creature for a sliver of humanity. She came up empty handed.

If her legs were in working order, Rahab knew she would have been running.

The small beast came close enough to sniff Rahab's head as she closed her eyes tight and waited for the thing to rip into her already aching flesh. She could hear the deep inhales closing in around her ears. She could feel its hot exhale on her forehead.

After one last huff, the creature let out a deafening cackle beside Rahab's left ear.

She opened her eyes, expecting to see the ugly face of the being staring down at her. To her surprise, it ran around in a circle beside her like a wild dog chasing its tail. It was still laughing.

Fear turned to anger as Rahab wanted nothing more than to kick the strange creature.

"Stupid human," the thing said, before it

disappeared behind a nearby building.

Rahab's bottom jaw hung open. The sound of the disgusting creature talking triggered a flash of images in her mind.

She *had* seen something like it before.

Faces rushed to her mind as Rahab recalled the events of the day.

Earlier that morning, she had been with her family enjoying the first meal of the day in their simple home. Rahab helped her mother clean up the dishes and got her younger brother, Noda, washed and ready for a nap.

Rahab began to sing a simple song to herself while she swept.

"Rahab, come in here." Her father's deep voice bellowed from the other side of the dark blue curtain which divided the large room.

She dropped the stick broom and rushed to him. Though Tzuri should have been gone for the day, Rahab didn't hesitate even for a moment when she heard her father call.

"There you are," he said, sitting in front of their small family altar to Astarte. His massive frame hid most of the altar from Rahab's view. Tzuri was a strong man and had seen much in his life. He worked with his hands and spoke little to anyone. Commands, along with any other interactions, were short and direct. He was a man who knew what he wanted and expected his family to fall in line behind him without question.

Rahab could tell he had been deep in prayer to

their goddess. The small oil lamp on the altar was lit. She could also see fresh flowers and food had been set around the small statue.

Without turning around, Tzuri spoke, "Rahab, I want you to know we finalized your marriage plans. When you come of age in a few years, you will be the wife of Kalil. He comes from a good family. You will be welcomed with anticipation."

Rahab nodded and bowed deeply.

Tzuri waved her off from his presence.

She picked up her broom and returned it to its place in the kitchen. Snatching a freshly cut flower from the table, Rahab ran outside to enjoy some fresh air.

Passing a street shrine, Rahab stopped to place the bright red pomegranate flower on the pile of offerings.

"Soon I'll be able to give so much more. Bless me, Astarte," she prayed. "Help me be a faithful woman and bear many children," she said, with a deep bow to the statue.

Familiar laughter behind her caught Rahab's attention. She turned around to see a group of friends playing.

"Guess what?" Rahab said, running up to them. "I'm getting married."

Two boys chuckled to each other.

"My father made my plans last year," one of the girls teased.

Rahab folded her arms across her chest.

"I think is it nice, Rahab," Gitel said.

"Thanks."

"Come, we're playing." She pulled on Rahab's folded arms.

One of the boys stepped up to Rahab, "Yes, you can have a turn being the dead person. Lie down on the ground and close your eyes."

Wanting to be included in the game, she did as he asked.

"Grab her," the boy screamed with glee.

Some of the children picked up Rahab as she tried to lie still. They carried her through the streets of Jericho.

One of the boys ran in front of them yelling, "Dead one coming through."

Another walked solemnly behind him, pretending to pray as he had seen the hooded men do during a real funeral procession.

The games went on as the sun crawled across the sky until it reached the distant mountains and hid behind them.

"I think I better go home now," Rahab called to Gitel.

"See you tomorrow," the young girl said as she waved to her friend and turned the corner with her older brother.

Rahab began to walk home. As she rounded a corner, she realized it was unfamiliar. Doubling back the way she had come, Rahab didn't see anything she recognized. She ambled up and down a few more streets to try to find her way in Jericho.

As darkness closed in, she could feel her heart start to beat faster as her breath quickened.

If I can find the temple fire, maybe I can find my way home.

All the stone buildings looked the same and each time she rounded a corner, the empty streets only taunted her with similarities. Pressing herself up against a nearby wall, Rahab looked around to find a face she could trust.

Though she could not see anyone, Rahab heard faint voices coming up the street.

"What now? I'm so bored," the first voice said.

"Let's see what else is around this city. Night has fallen and I'm sure we could find something to entertain us," a second voice called.

Rahab felt the hair on the back of her neck stand straight on end. Everything inside of her told her to run, but she was desperate to find help.

She took a cautious step closer to the edge of the building and peeked around the corner. Rahab covered her mouth to stifle a scream which threatened to erupt as she pulled her body back into the shadows.

Walking down the street were two large creatures that didn't belong in her world.

The first stood as tall as the double building he walked past. Horns poked out of every open place on his body. His skin was as red as a flame and his large eyes were set deep in his head. They were the darkest black Rahab had ever seen. Large pointed teeth stuck out of the creature's mouth in all directions. One of his arms was longer than the other, but the shorter arm was stouter. He walked with a slow gait and moved his head from side to side like an animal hunting its prey.

The second creature, equal in size, was covered with thin blades like those of a sickle. His skin was white with black splotches and large bumps. He had only one eye. Where the other should have been, a large curled claw stuck out of his head with the tip broken off.

"What are those things?" Rahab whispered to herself. "Goddess Astarte, hear your servant's plea. Give my feet wings to flee. Protect me, I pray." Rahab opened her eyes to find herself still pressed against the side of the building.

Astarte didn't hear her faint cries for help and Rahab could hear the hideous creatures coming closer.

"Where are all the men?" One of the beasts whined.

"I'm sure some will be along. This town is full of them," the other laughed.

The sound mixed with its echo off the stone walls. It was so loud that Rahab had to cover her ears until his laughter died down.

As her heart pounded faster, Rahab noticed two men rounding the corner of a nearby building. They were headed straight for the giant beasts.

Be careful. Why don't you see those awful creatures? Rahab screamed in her mind at the two men while she pressed herself harder against the wall. She was terrified that the creatures would see her.

The two men passed her without a backward glance.

Rahab peered around the corner and watched the men walk right through the creatures' massive legs.

They can't see them?

The eyes of each beast followed the men over their shoulders. They shared an evil glance with each other.

"They will do," the red one said.

Nodding his head, the white one extended his claw-like fingers and reached down to dig into the ground. He arched his back high into the air and let an ear-piercing howl escape from his drooling mouth.

Rahab pressed her hands over her ears, but they were already ringing from the noise.

The red creature pounded his chest before taking off at a full sprint.

Each creature reached his target at the exact same moment. They grabbed the heads of the two men to keep them from screaming. They were successful in not allowing a single sound to escape from the men's mouths.

Unfolding the muscles and flesh of the two, the creatures carefully ripped the bodies in half while they shrank in size to crawl inside the humans. Each disappeared completely into their covers and shook out their newly acquired limbs.

Upon gaining control, one turned to the other and began to laugh. "That is so much fun!"

"I'll say," the other agreed, shaking his head to clear out the fog.

The men cackled while they poked and punched at each other.

In the moments of mesmerizing fear, Rahab had left the safety of the building. She found herself standing in the middle of the street staring wide-eyed at the two possessed men.

The taller man's laughter stopped as he caught sight of Rahab. "Well, well, well. Time to have some fun."

The other man turned to see the girl frozen in horror. "Do you think she saw us?" he asked under his breath.

"Let's find out." Clearing his throat to allow his voice to drip like honey, the first man called out, "Hello there, my darling."

Rahab's muscles tightened.

"Looks like she did," he whispered to his partner.

The shorter man inhaled. "Do you smell that?"

The other nodded, but kept his eyes on Rahab.

"The fear is rolling off her in delicious waves."

"Don't be afraid, young one. We mean you no harm," the first one lied.

The two came close to Rahab and slithered around her like snakes surrounding a meal.

"What are you called?" The second man

asked.

Closing her eyes, Rahab hoped at any moment she would wake up from this nightmare and be safe in her home.

Help me, please! Astarte, where are you?

Warm tears streamed down her cheeks. She felt her knees begin to shake.

Save me, goddess Astarte.

When she opened her eyes, the two men were looking down at her with empty stares.

"Boo!" The first man yelled. His nose almost touched hers.

The second man reached out his hand to push her head covering until it fell to the ground. He wrapped some of Rahab's loose hair around his fingers and smelled. "Ah, a virgin. I do so love virgins."

A chill ran down Rahab's back at his cold touch.

"Not just a virgin. A young one on the edge of becoming a woman. Fresh and ripe for the picking. Such a delicious treat."

"We must hurry. We don't have much longer in these bodies," the other said. His body twitched.

"Are you thinking what I'm thinking?" the man asked, as he wrapped Rahab's hair tighter around his fingers until his hand made a fist. He pulled her frightened body close to his.

"Yes. Let's."

Each grabbed one of Rahab's arms as they

dragged her behind the building where she had been hiding. They began to rip at her clothes.

"Astarte!" Rahab shrieked as she pulled against their strength.

One of the men put his large hand over Rahab's mouth to muffle her screams. "Shh. Be a good girl and keep quiet."

Chapter 2

*"I am weary with my groaning; all the night make
I my bed to swim; I water my couch with my
tears."*
-PSALM 6:6

Tears stung Rahab's eyes as she relived the horrifying event in her mind. The pain in her body screamed in agreement with her thoughts. Violent sobs shook her delicate frame as she struggled to wipe the faces of the two men from her memory.

They would not leave.

Rahab released herself to the darkness that hung over her waiting to welcome her with open arms.

When Rahab stirred again, the darkness had given way to a bright white light mixed with hints of brown and blue. The pounding in her head had grown louder as the pulsing ache in her body grew stronger.

Voices called in the distance. Rahab couldn't make out what they were saying. The chill of fear ran up her back again as the commotion drew closer to her.

Words flew around her, but Rahab could not make them fit into a sentence she understood.

"...Girl..."

"...Dead..."

"...Blood..."

Rahab remembered the bright red flower she had placed at the feet of the street statue of her goddess.

Astarte? Why didn't you help me?

Tears rolled down her cheek.

Several voices spoke at once above her.

"...Help..."

"...Hurt..."

"...Help..."

"...Blood..."

"...Help..."

"...Dead..."

Rahab wanted to scream. She wanted to say anything to let the people whose faces crowded over her know she was alive. Every time she tried, her throat only gave up a soft rumble of misplaced noise.

Something warm covered her naked body.

A wave of shame crashed over her as her whole body burned red with embarrassment.

Before she knew it, strikes of pain flashed through her as she felt something hard and lumpy slip under her back. She could see the sky come close to her face and the buildings around her started to move.

As she passed a giant statue of Astarte, Rahab tried to reach for it.

Oh Goddess, hear your servant's plea...

But Astarte hadn't helped her. The goddess statue stood proud and still in the streets of Jericho with heaps of offerings at its feet.

Biting her lower lip to keep her stomach from turning over again, Rahab sunk back into the darkness.

Rahab had spent weeks recovering on her straw mat. Almost every bone in her body had been broken, including several ribs which hindered her breathing. Her once flawless medium-olive complexion was now covered with bruises of varying colors. Slashes of torn flesh were just beginning to mend. It took over a week before she could open her swollen eyes without pain.

As she lay on her mat one day, separated from the rest of the family, she overheard her parents talking.

"I know what she said," Rahab heard the deep voice of her father in the other room. "She must have done something to bring on that kind of act."

"But she's just a young girl. What could she

possibly have done to invite such wrath from the gods?" Her mother's voice was soft, but broken.

"I don't know, Liat. You did say she spent all day away from home. Maybe her and those friends of hers got into some trouble. Or maybe the gods were just punishing her laziness. She should have been here helping you with chores."

Rahab watched her parent's shadows move between the oil lamp and the sheer curtain.

"She's a good girl, Tzuri. Rahab wouldn't have gotten into trouble. What if she's telling the truth?"

"Truth?" Her father raised his voice. "Wild tales of night creatures as tall as buildings that no one else could see. Controlling men? You believe all those stories of hers? Nothing but lies to cover up whatever she did."

"I don't think she's lying. Why would she make up those kinds of stories?"

"Maybe she didn't like the arrangements I made for her marriage. Tried to get herself in trouble so we would call it off."

Liat huffed. "You know that girl practically worships you. She would have done anything to obey you. She trusts your judgment."

"Well, I don't know what to make of all this. She's got to be lying or losing her mind. I don't know which is worse."

"Have you heard from Kalil's family?"

"I'm meeting with them tomorrow," Tzuri sighed. "I fear the worst."

"As do I."

"Maybe I can make some kind of arrangement."

Rahab rolled to her side as she pulled her knees to her chest and covered her ears.

I'm not lying. I'm not...

She shook with frustration and anger. Hot tears stung her eyes, but she held them back.

After a long recovery, Rahab tried to sweep the dusty floor of her house as she fought to keep her eyes open. It had been weeks since she had slept through an entire night and the lack of restful sleep was catching up to Rahab. Her body slumped on the stick broom.

Noda's screams woke her.

"Shh..." Rahab picked up the child and rocked him. "There now. No more fussing."

Noda calmed in her arms.

She put him back down while she continued to clean.

Rahab came close to her family's altar. She picked up the small statue of Astarte. Rubbing her fingers over the carved places, Rahab gripped it tight in her hands. She closed her eyes and imagined smashing the idol to the ground.

Letting out her held breath, she placed the statue carefully back on the altar.

Returning to her sweeping, she glanced back at Astarte's stone expression.

You're not worth the punishment I'd get.

She looked over into a bowl of water. The places under her eyes were the darkest purple Rahab had ever seen. She rubbed her eyes and looked again. The reflection did not change. She kicked the bowl over.

"Rahab!" her mother scowled.

"Sorry,' she said, turning the bowl over. "I'll clean it up and fetch some more."

Rahab took a large clay jar to the local well.

"Rahab," Gitel's voice called to her.

Rahab waved.

"I haven't seen you in months."

Rahab nodded. She dipped her jug into the water.

"I miss you."

Rahab froze. "I'm sure your new husband will fill your days soon enough." She looked up to see Gitel gripping her empty jug. Tears began to form in her soft eyes.

"I'm sorry for what happened. I should have stayed with you."

"I need to get home," Rahab said as she turned away.

Tears burned in Rahab's eyes, but she wouldn't give them the satisfaction of release.

That night, Rahab laid her aching body on her straw mat.

Her family's gentle breathing echoed off the

stone walls of their small home.

Rahab closed her eyes.

The empty, black eyes of the two men and the flashes of broken flesh and screams erupted into violent dreams.

Rahab woke to her own screaming.

Her parents' heads perked up and gazed over at her.

"Not again," Tzuri said, as he rolled over.

"Try not to wake the baby, Rahab," Liat said with a yawn. She shook her head and moved closer to Tzuri.

"Yes, Mother." Rahab looked over at the sleeping Noda. She bit her lip and laid back down.

Within moments, Rahab heard her parent's steady breathing again. She stared at the ceiling and fought to calm her restless mind. Her tired body ached for relief that would only come with sleep.

Voices passed the open window.

Rahab watched the curtain blow with a mild breeze. Her whole body began to shake as beads of sweat pooled on her forehead. She kept her eyes wide open while she held her breath.

Exhaustion crept over Rahab's bony frame. She fought as hard as she could, but sleep threatened to overtake her again. With sleep, would come the faces. The faces would bring the screams as she relived, over and over again, the night she screamed for help that never came.

Chapter 3

> *"Yea, they sacrificed their sons and their*
> *daughters unto devils,"*
> -PSALM 106:37

While seasons changed to welcome new buds and plants, Rahab's thoughts wandered to the upcoming ritual sacrifice. The hooded men had always held such an interest in her young mind and she looked forward to the day with anticipation.

As the family went about their activities, Rahab overheard her mother and father speaking.

"Even is too old," her father's harsh voice insisted.

"I know. Why do they want one of our children anyway?" Rahab heard her mother's voice crack.

"It is a privilege to be chosen. The gods will be angry with us for turning down such an opportunity."

Rahab heard a loud pound.

Silence filled the next few moments.

Rahab went to move away, guessing her father

had finished the discussion. She heard her mother's voice again.

"Why not Rahab?" Liat's voice was so faint Rahab thought she had misunderstood.

Rahab heard a deep sigh, but couldn't tell from which parent it came.

"We chose her when she was born, remember?" Her mother's voice was light. "You said 'she would make an excellent sacrifice child if they ever asked.' Those were your words."

"I know what I said."

"So, why not Rahab instead of Noda?" her mother's voice demanded.

Noda? The hooded men were asking for Noda? Yes, why not me? Rahab stomped her foot.

Her thoughts ran back through the few times she had been allowed to watch the great spring sacrifice. When the little ones walked up to the hooded figure and were lifted up high in the air, the looks on their parents' faces were always of pride. Rahab wanted to put that look back on her own parents' faces.

A tear welled up at the corner of her eye. She remembered the look of fear and disappointment on her parents' faces the night her body was brought back. She was bloody, bruised, and ruined.

Rahab shook the memory away.

She turned to see her sweet younger brother, Noda, playing on the floor with a stone and a stick.

He giggled to himself.

Take me. Please take me instead of him. She hung her head and let a single tear slide down her cheek.

"Because she's no longer pure," her father said.

Rahab's mouth hung open as her head flew up in the direction of the voices.

She heard her mother gasp. "The incident? They're blaming it on her?"

"It doesn't matter how it happened," Tzuri boomed, then lowered his voice. "They only care *that* it happened to her. Since she's no longer a virgin; she's not an acceptable sacrifice. The elders are afraid that if they give her up, the gods will be angry. It is the first sacrifice of the coming bloom. We need to bring our best offering."

"I won't let them take my Noda," Rahab heard her mother's voice come close to the thick curtain.

"You don't have a choice."

Rahab made her hands busy as her mother hurried into the room.

Liat scooped Noda up in her arms and headed outside.

Rahab turned to look into her father's face which had appeared just inside the room.

Tzuri watched Liat disappear out the front door and turned his gaze toward Rahab. He sighed and then pulled his head back through the curtain.

Rahab collapsed.

They didn't pick me.

Her shoulders shook. Heat rose through Rahab like she had never felt before. Her fists tightened by her side. A scream crawled its way up her throat, but she fought it down. She looked over at her family's beloved Astarte statue.

I hate you.

The statue's slight smile only fanned the flames of hatred that grew in Rahab's heart. Her mind raced with thoughts of her brother's young face.

I have to save him. I have to save both of us.

Late the following evening, as her parents prepared the other children for sleep, Rahab picked up the shoulder bag she had packed earlier. She grabbed Noda and ran for the front door.

She made it several steps down the street before running straight into a neighbor woman.

"What are you doing out here this late, young one? These streets are no place for you."

"Sorry. I'm just on my way home..."

"Now, you just wait. Are you trying to steal that little boy there?" The woman pulled on Rahab's arm.

The jolt caused Noda to cry out.

"No. He's my brother. We're going home," Rahab said, as she pulled away from the woman and tried to soothe the boy at the same time.

"He belongs to those people there." The woman pointed to Rahab's house. "Give him here," she demanded, pulling on the crying boy.

"Let go. He's my brother. Let him go," Rahab screamed.

"What is going on?" Tzuri pulled the two

women apart and snatched Noda out of Rahab's arms.

"This one here," the woman said, shaking her bony finger in Rahab's face. "She's trying to steal that little boy of yours."

Tzuri pulled the veil off Rahab's head and looked into the freighted eyes of his daughter. "Rahab? What are you doing with your brother?"

"I'm trying to save him from the fire," she bawled.

Her father looked at his two crying children. "Thank you," he said to the older woman and gathered his son and daughter. Taking them inside his home, he handed Noda to Liat before leading Rahab to the next room. Making her sit down, Tzuri paced the room several times before he spoke, "I know your intentions were pure, daughter, but you cannot go around stealing your siblings."

She wanted to interrupt her father and explain herself. Rahab knew doing so would get her a slap across the mouth for speaking out of turn.

"If you had come to me or your mother, we would have explained," Tzuri continued. "What got into that head of yours? You know the penalty for stealing." He stopped and looked at his quiet daughter. "Well?"

Rahab kept her head down. "I heard you tell Mother you were going to offer Noda instead of me."

"Daughter, it is a privilege to be chosen as a

sacrifice child." Tzuri knelt on the ground in front of her. "We are happy to have one of our dear ones be given over to win the favor of the gods."

"Why Noda?" Rahab slipped. She recoiled in anticipation of a slap.

Tzuri reached out to lift Rahab's delicate chin up so her eyes met his. "I think you are old enough to hear the truth." He sat on the floor. "Noda is the purest of our children and so will be the one the gods will accept."

"Mother said you picked me first."

"Yes, it's true." Tzuri scooped up his daughter and placed her in his lap. "When you were born, you were the most beautiful little thing I had ever seen." He tilted her head up again so he could look into her face. "Those eyes of yours shone like amber hardened in the sun. And your skin was so pure. When I first saw you, I thought you were a goddess sent down to us from above." He brushed some hair out of her eyes and wiped away the tear streaks from her cheeks.

Placing her veil back on her head, he wrapped it carefully around her neck. "Your mother and I decided that very day if the elders ever came to us for a child, you would be the best sacrifice anyone could ever give. Then when those *men...*," he spat the word out, "...hurt you. Our choice was taken away. We could not risk handing you over and having the gods be angry with us. I know it wasn't your fault. Sometimes things happen to us beyond our control and all we can do is move forward.

Noda is still young and the most acceptable child in our family. He must be the one." Tzuri kissed his daughter's head and placed Rahab back on her feet. "Now, be a good girl and get ready to sleep," he said and left the room.

Rahab glanced over at her rolled-up straw mat.

"Sleep?" she whispered. "I wish I never had to sleep again." She shuddered.

The family spent days preparing Noda for the coming ritual. Each day, they took extra care to clean him and feed him first.

When the day came for the sacrifice, the family headed to the temple.

Rahab heard loud voices coming from the front of a large crowd ahead of her.

"Who is speaking, Mother?"

"Those are the elders, Rahab. They are praying. They are asking that the sacrifices we are about to make would be welcomed and the gods would bless us with a large harvest," her mother said, as she pushed her way through the crowd.

Tzuri had made it to the front with Noda in his arms ahead of the rest of the family.

One of the hooded men was there waiting. He took the young child and placed him in line behind three other children.

Rahab noticed the bright fire burning in the

large altar bowl. She had seen it many times in passing as her mother took her to the market street. The closer she got, the larger it appeared.

Liat, Even, and Rahab found a place in the crowd to watch the ceremony begin.

One of the hooded men reached down and picked up the first waiting child. A little girl whose straight black hair had been brushed until it shone in the sunlight.

The man held her high in the air and waved her body over the crowd and then to the small group of elders who nodded their hoods in approval. He tossed her into the waiting flame.

Short shrieks erupted from the altar bowl before Rahab could no longer hear the little girl's cries.

Placing the next two children into the fire in the same manner, the hooded man reached for Noda.

Rahab looked up to her mother's face.

"Mother?"

Liat was intently watching the ritual.

Rahab pressed closer to the front. Balancing on her tiptoes, she watched between the group of people in front of her.

Noda smiled at the man. He lifted his chubby, little arms up to the hooded figure.

Rahab looked from Noda to the altar bowl and back again.

Wait.

The praying man stepped closer to the bowl.

No. Wait!

Rahab tried to squeeze her thin frame between the watchers.

"Noda!" She reached for her brother.

The man heaved Noda into the fire as he repeated a prayer.

Noda's screams made their way to Rahab's ears as she covered them in horror.

"Get him out of there!" She managed to press herself through the crowd and fell at the feet of the hooded man.

Rahab felt her stomach turn over as the smell of her brother's burning flesh hit her nose. She grabbed her stomach and leaned over to allow her morning meal to flee her mouth.

She looked up into the dark eyes peering at her from under the dark material.

He shook his head and turned away.

Wiping her chin with the back of her hand, Rahab twisted to her unsteady feet. She picked up the hem of her dress and ran toward home.

She flung open the front door and rushed up to the rooftop. Tears flooded her eyes and her body shook.

When she reached the rooftop, she looked out at the busy city of Jericho. The smoke from the altar fire was billowing towards the sky.

Rahab turned her back.

"Oh, Noda. What have they done to you?" she wept.

She slid down the edge of the half wall. Pulling

her legs up to her chest, Rahab wrapped her arms around herself. She let the tears roll down her warm cheeks. She buried her head into her knees and rocked herself.

As the sun moved across the blue sky, Rahab heard footsteps coming up the stairs.

She looked up to see her mother standing on the top step.

"Daughter, I have some disappointing news to share with you."

"Yes, Mother?"

Liat took a deep breath and let out a heavy sigh. "I'm afraid your marriage proposal has been withdrawn."

Rahab let her shoulders fall as all the air left her body.

"I know what happened to you was not your fault. It happened and we can't take it back."

"Wh...what...?" Rahab tried to take a breath to steady herself, but the air would not fill her lungs. "What am I to do now?" she asked, looking to the floor.

Liat stared at her for several moments. "There are not many choices left." Her mother rubbed her newly growing belly. "We needed to restore favor to this family."

Rahab looked into the downcast eyes of her mother.

"What are you saying?"

Tzuri huffed behind Liat. He stepped around her. "What we're saying, Rahab, is that we didn't have much choice. We spoke to the temple leaders after the ceremony. They are willing to purchase you so we can cleanse our family from your disgrace."

"Sell me?" Rahab tilted her head at her father.

"Yes. They are expecting you before dark. You'll serve in the temple until they feel you have fulfilled your obligation."

"Obligation?"

"It was enough of a disgrace for you to become impure. Then you go and dishonor us at the ceremony today like you did." He waved toward the temple smoke.

"Father, I didn't mean..."

"Enough." He raised a hand to silence her. "Get your things together. We leave soon."

The sun hung low in the sky, as Rahab ambled behind her parents to the temple of Astarte.

The large mud-brick structure rose over the horizon.

Rahab looked up to see the large altar bowl come into view.

Noda's screams still rung in her ears. She covered them and began to weep.

"Keep up, Rahab," Tzuri called without turning around.

People moved everywhere around the temple.

Rahab's feet drug under her.

"Ahh, Tzuri. Good to see you again. Liat, a pleasure." A man dressed in a long, white robe kissed the cheeks of her parents. "And this must be

Rahab."

Rahab stared up at the old man.

Tzuri cleared his throat.

Looking down, Rahab bowed.

"Everything is arranged," the elder said, handing Tzuri a cloth bag tied at the top. "I'll give you a moment."

Liat hugged Rahab. "Stay safe. Please be obedient."

"Try not to get yourself into trouble," Tzuri said, as he headed for the open court.

Liat followed.

"Mother, how can you do this?" Rahab ran after her.

She stopped, but didn't turn around.

"How could you kill Noda and now sell me? How!" Rahab fell at her mother's feet.

"Get up," Tzuri ordered. "You will do as you are told."

"Mother?" Rahab whined.

Tzuri grabbed Rahab's arm and pulled her up to her feet. He dragged her over to the man and placed her arm into his hand. "You'll do best to find your lot in this world. Astarte doesn't look too kindly on women who don't know their place."

"Father, please let me come home," Rahab wept. "I'll do anything. Please?"

Tzuri turned his back and left with Liat.

"Father!"

"Enough, girl." The priest led her by the arm into the temple.

Rahab sobbed.

The man took her into a room filled with beautifully dressed women. "Mirit," he called.

A dark-haired woman, adorned with jewels, approached them. "Yes?"

"Here." The old priest held out Rahab's arm. "Got a new one for you. Train her well."

Mirit took Rahab's arm and nodded.

As soon as he left, Mirit let Rahab go. "It's alright, young one. I'm going to take good care of you."

Rahab sniffled and looked up into her eyes.

"There now. That's better." Mirit patted her head. "I'm called Mirit, what's your name?"

"Rahab."

"Rahab, huh? Should call you Honey with those eyes." She laughed. "Paebel didn't hurt you too bad, did he?" She reached for Rahab's arm.

Rahab jerked away and rubbed her aching arm. She shook her head.

"Well, let's get you changed. Can't go around here looking like a peasant."

Rahab looked down at her dirty, brown dress.

"Maybe we can find something to match those eyes of yours."

Chapter 4

"Do not prostitute thy daughter, to cause her to be a whore; lest the land fall to whoredom, and the land become full of wickedness."
-LEVITICUS 19:29

Rahab limped behind Mirit through the crowded streets of the market.

"Still sore?" Mirit asked.

"Yes, a little."

Mirit nodded. "You'll get used to it. We'll get some more salve while we're out."

They browsed at each booth picking up a few odds and ends for themselves and some for the other temple priestesses.

"It's nice to get out in the fresh air," Rahab said, as she turned her face towards the rays of early morning sun.

Mirit watched the temple guards who stayed close.

"Yes. Even a few moments of freedom are worth it."

Rahab looked to the two large men. "They're not so bad."

Mirit stopped at the next booth. She picked up a jade necklace and held it to her neck in admiration.

"It's nice, but you've got lots of nicer ones at the temple."

Mirit sighed as she ran the beads through her fingers. "Nothing there belongs to me. All of those decorations belong to the temple. When my time is up, they'll kick me out with little more than a simple dress."

"They wouldn't do that to you," Rahab protested. "You're the greatest priestess we have."

Mirit shook her head. "You have much to learn, young one."

An unusual smell caught Rahab's nose and she found herself drawn to it. At the next booth, she found a large pile of dried leaves. Digging her fingers into the pile, Rahab brought a handful to her nose and inhaled its scent. "What is this?"

The merchant man turned toward her. "Chamomile. Helps with sleep."

"Really?"

He nodded.

"We use it sometimes at the temple," Mirit said, joining her.

"For what?"

"It helps men relax." Mirit caught the eyes of the merchant. "Some men need it."

The large man huffed and turned toward his other customer.

Rahab inhaled the small pile in her hands

again. "It's wonderful."

Mirit leaned over to her ear and whispered, "It also keeps the big ones under control."

Rahab tilted her head.

Pulling a coin from her pouch, Mirit handed it to the merchant who had turned back to them. "We'll take some."

The man scooped and poured a small pile into a cloth pouch before handing it to Mirit.

Rahab dusted the leaves from her hands back onto the large pile.

"Come, I'll show you."

Back at the temple, Mirit brought a small pot of water to a boil. "While the water is getting nice and hot, crush up a few of those leaves there. Only a few."

Rahab obeyed.

"Yes. Now, when the water boils, remove it from the fire and add the powder. Let it steep for a few minutes." She poured the warm liquid into a small cup. "And there we have it. Make the big ones drink this and they will be wet clay in your hands."

Watching the steam rise from the cup, Rahab inhaled the scent. "Can I try it?"

"I don't see the harm. It's not very strong."

Rahab picked up the cup and took a careful sip. "It doesn't taste as good as it smells."

Mirit nodded. "But it gets the job done."

The tightly wound muscles in Rahab's body began to unwind. Her shoulders slouched and her breathing eased.

"Told you. Works well if you get it right."

Rahab's head popped up. "What if you get it wrong?"

"Nothing really," Mirit said, as she began to clean up. "It's not like it could kill you or anything. If you make it too strong, it would only put you to sleep for a while."

Rahab looked down into the cup. "How strong would you have to make it?"

"Why?"

Rahab shrugged. "You know, if you have trouble sleeping."

"I told you I'd help you put some salve on later."

"No, not from that. I mean..."

"The screaming?"

Rahab's cheeks grew hot. "You hear me?"

"I think the whole temple hears you muffling your screaming into your blankets at night. We've just gotten used to it by now."

"Oh." Rahab took another sip. "Nightmares."

"Like wild creatures chasing you?"

Rahab flinched. "You could say so."

"I thought only kids had nightmares. Figured you'd have grown out of them by now. I mean I know it's a lot when you first come here and all the *training*..."

Flashes of sweaty men raced across Rahab's mind. "No, not the training. Before I came here..."

"I see."

"When I was a kid," Rahab said as she downed the last of the liquid. She handed the empty cup to Mirit. "Thanks for showing me how to make it."

"Happy to share. I think you needed it."

"Why do you say that?"

"You know. To help you relax. For later."

Rahab shrugged.

"They didn't tell you?"

"Tell me what?"

"The king is coming to see you tonight."

Rahab felt the warmth leave her cheeks. "The king of Jericho?"

"No, the king of the gods. Yes, the king of Jericho."

"Coming here to see me?"

"Yes," Mirit said. "You don't look so good. You should go take a nap before the king gets here."

Rahab shook her head. "No. I'll be fine."

"I really think you should go lay down for a while. I'll come wake you up before he arrives."

The room spun around Rahab. She grabbed her head. "Maybe you're right. I think I'll go lay down."

"Rahab."

She felt her shoulder shake.

"Rahab. The king will be here soon. Time to

wake."

"I'm awake," Rahab yawned and rolled over.

Mirit shook her again. "Rahab."

She sat up. "Yes. Yes."

Mirit moved around the room. "I'll get your room ready for the king. You go get yourself ready."

Rahab got up and reached for a nearby piece of polished brass. She brushed out the knots in her hair and cleaned up her face.

"He'll be here any moment," Mirit said, as she adjusted Rahab's clothes.

"What do I need to know?"

"He likes to lead. Let him. He also likes to talk. Let him."

"Anything else?"

"Remember, he's the king. Do what he says. No matter what. Unless you want your head on a platter tonight."

Rahab shuddered.

Loud footsteps came close to her door.

"The soldiers. He doesn't go anywhere without a company of guards." Mirit brushed some wrinkles from Rahab's dress. "Luckily, they stay outside the door."

"Luckily?"

"You don't want to know what they like to do."

A knock came.

"Enter," Mirit said, moving to stand in front of Rahab.

She peered through Mirit's arm. A man

dressed in the finest robes Rahab had ever seen stepped into the room. His beard was just beginning to gray. His broad shoulders matched the frame of the door. He wasn't exceedingly handsome to look at, but his presence made Rahab's knees weak.

"Your Majesty," Mirit sang. "May I present to you, Rahab. One of our finest priestesses for your pleasure this evening." She stepped to the side with a deep bow and waved toward Rahab.

Rahab bowed low.

The king nodded his head with a slight movement.

"I shall leave you two, my king." Mirit bowed again and left the room.

"Please," Rahab waved to the bed.

After some time together, Rahab laid down next to the king.

"Have you heard the stories of the group of people from the south?"

"The Wanderers, my king?"

"Yes," he said. Adjusting himself on the blankets, he went on, "They used to be Egyptian slaves. It seems they escaped by crossing the Red Sea on dry land. Completely dry. Like the desert sand when the sun is at its highest in the sky." The king chuckled to himself. "Dry land? Have you ever heard such nonsense?"

"No, my king."

"The sea stood on either side of them waiting for them to pass." He gestured with his hands for emphasis. "When all their people crossed over, the Egyptian army tried to follow after. The sea crushed them. Wiping out all of the warriors."

Rahab's mouth hung open. "All of them?"

"Yes. Anyway, it seems their god shows up as a pillar of cloud by day and a pillar of fire by night. It leads them around the desert." He belly laughed. "To top it off, every morning when they get up there is white stuff on the ground outside of their tents. They pick it and eat it. They call it manna. Oh, how these stories keep me smiling."

"Yes, my king."

The king stood and redressed himself.

Rahab bowed as the king left her room.

She heard a quick knock a moment later. "Enter."

Mirit stepped in. "How did it go?"

"You were right. He does like to talk."

"What did he talk about?" Mirit sat on the bed.

"The Wanderers."

Mirit rolled her eyes. "His favorite topic."

Chapter 5

"And, behold, there met him a woman with the attire of an harlot, and subtil of heart."
-PROVERBS 7:10

1406 B.C.

Years flew as Rahab's popularity among the temple customers grew. Her youthful frame filled out into a well-devolved woman. Word spread far and wide about the beautiful temple priestess.

One day, a tall man robed in fine linens came to the temple of Astarte in Jericho.

"I'm looking for the one called Rahab," he stated.

"Of course, you are," one of the girls said under her breath. "This way, please."

The man was lead to a private room.

"He's next," the younger girl called to Rahab through the open door.

"You're not from Jericho, are you?" Rahab asked, noticing the fine garments and foreign features of the man.

"No, I come from Gibeon." He smiled as he circled her. "I'm a very important man there; an Ambassador."

"I bet you are," she said. "First order of business, your offer."

He pulled a coin bag from his belt and dumped several coins into Rahab's open hand.

"It's enough," she said as she placed the payment into her own bag. "What are you called, Ambassador?"

"Ahio."

"Make yourself comfortable over there." She pointed across the room.

He complied.

"Drink this." Rahab handed him a small cup of tea.

"What is this? I don't drink anything my guards have not tasted first," he said, standing to fetch one.

"Then you don't get me."

Ahio froze in his steps and looked down at the steamy liquid. "What is it?"

Rahab turned to him and smiled. "Just something to make you more comfortable."

He raised an eyebrow at her and then looked back down at the cup. Lifting it to his mouth, he swallowed the tea in one quick gulp.

"Good. Now, go lie back down," she ordered.

After an hour, the man rolled onto his back and let out a deep sigh of relief. "You *are* as good as they say."

"People talk too much."

"As do kings."

Rahab tilted her head.

"Just the other day, the king of Gibeon himself was going on about this group of people he is growing concerned about." He put his arms under his head. "My king said he heard they are larger than they are rumored to be. They have been walking around in the desert for decades. Multiplying and following the signs of their god. He called them..."

"Wanderers?"

"Yes. You've heard of them?"

"Many speak of them."

"They've just been walking around out there. I wonder if they are waiting for something," Ahio thought aloud.

"Well, what makes your king worry so much. If they are just a bunch of wanderers?"

"Their numbers are what put fear in the heart of my king and several others as a matter of fact. And the stories of the power their god has displayed."

"What stories has he told?"

"He told me these people used to be slaves in Egypt, building tombs for the Pharaoh. Could you imagine? A group of slaves, led by a crazy old man, rose up against such a capable man as the ruler of all Egypt."

"Maybe the Pharaoh wasn't as strong as everyone believed."

"The Pharaoh's are practically gods. The Wanderers' god cursed the whole country and brought nothing but plagues on the land and the people. Finally, Pharaoh gave in and sent them away." The Ambassador laughed. "They've been wandering around in the desert ever since." He rolled over and ran his fingers over Rahab's bare stomach. "Still, my king is worried about them."

"Why?" Rahab wondered honestly for the first time and surprised even herself with the question.

He grinned. "Seems they follow a pretty powerful god."

The words rang in Rahab's mind long after Ahio left.

A powerful god.

She considered the gods and goddesses her people served. They didn't seem to have any power. All they did was request children to be burned in exchange for not actively bringing harm to the crops. It did not seem like much power to Rahab or, at the very least, a gross misuse of such; to only have favor by bribery. She had given up on winning them over.

Several months later, the Ambassador returned.

"Hello, Rahab."

She turned to see the dark, bearded face of Ahio. Smiling, she held out her delicate hand with her palm facing up.

Ahio laughed. "Right to business. I do love that about you."

After she had done all she could to please him physically, Rahab remained silent.

Ahio laid down beside her.

Knowing the Ambassador would slip into a conversation. Rahab made herself comfortable. She hoped their talk would lead to more about the Wanderers, as she liked to think of the people who wakened such fear in the hearts of men and kings alike.

"I spent most of yesterday lounging by the pools. The week of meetings had tired me to the point of much-needed rest." He chuckled to himself as Rahab's attention entered the conversation already in progress.

She waited, but Ahio never spoke of the people in the desert. Taking matters into her own hand, Rahab spoke up, "Has your king grown tired of the people who wander in the desert?"

Ahio looked over at Rahab. "Why do you ask?"

"Oh, just curiosity." She sat up and reached over for her dress. "You have not spoken of them yet. I thought maybe your king had done something about them."

"No, he chooses not to waste his energy on those who do not pose an immediate threat to his throne," he said as he watched her.

"Oh, I see."

"Would you like to hear another story about

them?" Ahio asked.

She nodded slightly.

"My king says they carry around a gold box covered in a blue, wool cloth."

Rahab tilted her head. "A gold box?"

"Yes."

"What's inside?"

"Their laws, I think. They claim their god wrote down their laws on two stone tablets and they made the box to carry them around. The thing is supposed to have power of its own, hence the reason for the cover."

"Power?"

"Apparently, it has killed before."

She squinted at Ahio, half believing him and half considering if he was making up stories to keep her attention. "The box killed someone?"

"Yes, rumor says two men tried to offer idols to it and they were struck dead. Then one day, a man helping transport it, reached out to steady it and he was burned to death by the box."

She rolled over onto her back and stared up at the ceiling. Rahab was done listening to tales about people who were senseless enough to wander aimlessly in the desert carrying a box of death.

"Come with me," Ahio offered, as he twirled her black hair around his finger.

Looking sideways at him, Rahab took a deep breath. She didn't know if it was the tea talking or if the man's power stayed in his head so much that he thought whatever he asked for would be his without question. Whatever it was, Rahab didn't want to trade one set of obligations for another.

"I can't."

"Can't or won't?" he asked, as he rose to stand over her.

Rahab stood to finish dressing in silence.

"Fine," Ahio huffed. "Die a wretch in this misery-soaked city. Don't you ever come crawling to me."

She stood with her back toward him.

"I will be back," Ahio said. He threw on his outer robe.

She watched over her shoulder as he walked out the door.

I know.

Chapter 6

*"For jealousy is the rage of a man: therefore he
will not spare in the day of vengeance."*
-PROVERBS 6:34

Rahab walked the crowded streets of Jericho
toward the marketplace. It had been months since
she entertained Ahio or the king of Jericho. The
break was welcomed. The money was missed.

Various smells of spices and animals filled her
nose. The sounds of people conducting their daily
business entertained her ears.

Wandering from booth to booth, she looked
up to see the familiar face of her own mother.
Lucky for Rahab, her mother had not seen her.
Then Rahab's eyes found the young face of her
sister.

Alma.

Rahab hid among the crowd as she followed
them to get a closer look.

"Stay close, Alma," Liat called.

"Yes, Mother."

It is her.

Though Rahab had not been allowed to be

part of her family as she served in the Temple, she still saw her family grow. They frequented to Temple of Astarte often to offer sacrifices and present offerings. Each new child that joined her family was brought to the Temple to be blessed by the priests. She had seen all of them grow from afar and many start their own families.

Will she even recognize me?

Moving closer, Rahab grabbed Alma's arm.

Alma fought back and let out a loud scream.

Rahab covered her sister's mouth with one hand and held her finger up to her own lips with the other. "Shh. It's me. Rahab. Your sister."

Alma's eyes widened.

Rahab slowly removed her hand from the young girl's mouth.

"Rahab?"

She nodded.

Alma wrapped her arms around her sister. "Rahab!"

"Shh!" Rahab pushed her arms away.

Covering her own mouth, Alma whispered, "Sorry. Oh, Rahab. I can't believe it's you. Mother will be so thrilled..." Alma said, looking around.

"Alma, listen, go back to Mother. But don't tell her you saw me. Can you get away later?"

"I can try."

"Good. Come to Astarte's Temple."

"Alma?" Liat called.

"Coming, Mother," Alma said over her shoulder.

"Do you think you can find it?" Rahab asked.

"Yes, I know it."

"Good girl." Rahab patted her shoulder. "Go now and remember, don't tell Mother."

A knock at her door let Rahab know her next customer had arrived.

Hopefully the last for today.

"Enter," she called.

The door opened slowly and in stepped a large man.

Rahab squinted to see the face of Ahio.

"Greetings, beautiful," he said.

She rolled her eyes, but she knew she would be a fool to turn away her highest paying customer. "May I help you?"

"Sure thing." He closed the door behind himself and tossed a bag of coins in her direction.

She caught the bag with one hand, opened it, and counted the coins. It was a similar amount to what he had always paid. Rahab knew it meant he wanted to talk, but first he would want to be satisfied.

"Come with me," Ahio said, placing Rahab's hand on his broad, hairy chest after their time together.

Rahab groaned as she pulled her hand away. "We've been over this."

"But I could make you so happy. I know I could."

Rahab pulled her dress over her head. "It's not about happiness."

"Then what is it?"

Rahab froze.

"You know only one of two things will happen in this temple. Either you will rot here being served up on a golden platter to the highest bidder. Or your body will betray you as your looks fade like the dunes. Then they will put you out on the streets. What then? Would you rather die a beggar than be with me?"

She kept her back to him.

"You are so infuriating, Rahab. I can offer you the world," he said, dressing quickly. "I have a good mind to teach you a lesson."

"Leave, Ahio." She pointed to the door.

He caught her hand. "Oh, I will, but not without you. Guards."

Two large men came into the room.

"She's coming with us. Be careful not to harm her."

One of the men wrapped Rahab up in his arms.

Rahab screamed as he lifted her in the air and carried her out of the room.

The guard managed to get a hand over her mouth to muffle her screams.

Her mind flashed with images of the two creatures. She screamed under his hand and kicked hard. Her foot found its target and the man dropped her.

Rahab ran toward her room.

"Get back here," the other guard called as he caught her.

She clawed at his arm and dug her heels into the floor.

"Keep her quiet," Ahio ordered.

The guard threw Rahab up over his shoulder.

"What's going on here?" Mirit said, stepping in front of them. "Put her down."

Ahio pushed past her. "Out of the way."

Mirit followed. "Put her down at once. I will call the temple guard," she demanded.

"What is the meaning of all this noise?" The old priest named Paebel stopped the group.

"Here, this should cover it," Ahio said, handing the man a large bag.

"What are you talking about?" Paebel asked.

"I'm taking this woman with me. She's close to her service time anyway. I'm sure you'll find a more than adequate payment there." He motioned to the bag. "If not, I can send more."

Paebel opened the bag. "There is quite a lot of money here. Rahab is one of our best women. I'm sure the other priests aren't going to be happy to see her go."

"Listen," Ahio said as he leaned in close to the man, "I'm sure we can come to some kind of agreement. Like I said, her service is almost up as it is and I'm sure your goddess would be more than happy with such a large offering. It's probably more than this one woman," he waved to Rahab, "could bring in for the rest of her time."

"Indeed," he said, looking back into the bag.

Ahio motioned for his guards to follow him.

"You can't let this happen," Mirit said.

"This generous man has paid for a poor woman who was about to be put out on the streets," Paebel said. "You should be thanking him."

" 'Thanking him'?" Mirit huffed. "He's stealing her."

"No, there is no crime here. See..." he said, holding out the bag, "...payment in full."

Rahab screamed another muffled scream under the guard's hand.

"Try to keep quiet about it,' Paebel called. "I don't want the whole temple woken up."

Ahio ordered Rahab to be taken to his waiting caravan.

Once they arrived at his luxurious home in Gibeon, Ahio had his guards change Rahab into different clothes.

"There now. You look more like a respectful woman of Gibeon. Better than some temple prostitute," Ahio said, admiring her.

"I am a temple prostitute," she said.

"Not anymore, my dear. You're all mine now. Sold as my concubine and for my pleasure." He came near her and wrapped her long hair around his finger. "We are going to have so much fun."

She spat in his face.

Ahio reached back and slapped her. "You'll do well to learn your new place, woman."

Rahab rubbed her stinging cheek.

"Bind her hands," he ordered.

Rahab kept her glare on Ahio as the men wrapped cords around her hands.

"Watch that pretty little mouth of yours," he said, gripping her cheek in one hand and squeezing. "Or I'll have to add a gag as well."

Chapter 7

"For by means of a whorish woman a man is brought to a piece of bread: and the adulteress will hunt for the precious life."
-PROVERBS 6:26

"Hello, my beautiful oasis," Ahio called, entering Rahab's room.

Rahab pressed her lips together.

"Still bitter?" He said, edging closer to her. "I thought you would have softened by now. It's been months."

She crossed her arms.

"Have I not given you everything?" Ahio nuzzled her neck. "Food, wine, and the finest dresses wages can purchase."

Rahab huffed.

Ahio wrapped his arm around her waist and pulled her tight into himself. "I've given you everything a woman's heart could imagine. Yet you're still as cold as the marble statues that line the palace halls."

He leaned down and kissed her hard.

She tensed under his weight.

"Nothing?" he asked, searching her eyes. "I see." Ahio shoved her.

Rahab stumbled, but managed to catch herself on one knee.

"If I didn't need that pretty face of yours tonight, you'd be getting worse right now."

Rahab perked up.

Ahio grabbed her chin and twisted it. "Such a shame. All that beauty fashioned to a stone will."

She fought the urge to spit in his face.

"No matter." He pushed her face away. "In time, you shall bend to my will."

"Maid," he called.

An older woman entered the room with her gaze toward the floor.

"Get her prepared for tonight. Take your time." He looked back at Rahab. "I want her to shine brighter than the brightest jewels in the king's treasury." With that, Ahio left the room.

"Mistress." The woman rushed over to Rahab and put a hand under Rahab's elbow. "Are you injured?"

"No, Tahirah." Rahab held up her free hand. "Peace."

Tahirah helped Rahab to her feet.

Rahab grabbed for her stinging knee.

"Let me take a look." She helped Rahab sit on a nearby couch.

"I'm sure it's nothing."

Tahirah rubbed Rahab's knee gently.

Rahab winced.

"I think it will heal quickly." She fetched a small bottle and some fresh linens from across the room. "Let's wrap it up."

Rahab nodded. "What's planned for tonight?"

Tahirah paused for a moment and then continued wrapping. "Mistress, you know I..."

"I know you well enough to know you hear all talk that flies through this place."

She smiled for a moment. "You are smarter than Master Ahio believes."

"As are you."

"There is to be a great feast in your honor tonight. Master Ahio has invited many of his friends and other palace officials. To meet the 'prize of Jericho' as he calls you." She finished wrapping Rahab's knee and returned the items to their proper place.

"To be put on display."

"In a sense. You know men like to show off who's treasures are grander."

"I do not wish to be a displayed treasure."

"Mistress," Tahirah cleared her throat. "Am I free to speak?"

"Yes," Rahab said, patting the space next to her on the couch.

Tahirah rushed to her side. "I've heard talk among the guards that you've been asking questions."

Rahab stiffened.

"You've asked about their routines and any weakness in their protection."

"Merely wanting to protect myself." Rahab straightened her shoulders.

"I see." Tahirah wiped her hands on her worn dress. "Well, if one wanted to know if there were any weakness in the guard, then one should ask someone who has been here a very long time."

"Someone who would know all the guards well and how they move?" Rahab softened.

"Oh, yes. Someone wise beyond her years and worn by the treatment of an ignorant Master. Someone who might know of a perfect time, like tonight. When the guards will be more concerned about people coming in than they will be about someone leaving."

Rahab rose and then stumbled.

"Someone who also might have to figure out a way to steal a horse." She chuckled.

"I would be forever in your debt." Rahab rubbed her wrapped knee.

"We've got to be smart though. I'll get some of the other ladies to help me get you ready for tonight. We'll have plenty to spare. Master Ahio always hires more for feasts." She helped Rahab sit on the couch. "Rest, Mistress. I have plans to make."

"Maybe we should wait until I can flee on my own. Won't stealing a horse be too much?"

"Yes, it will be work," she said, holding her pointed chin. "Though we won't have another opportunity like this soon."

Rahab thought on the past months. "What do

you need me to do?"

"Rest. Be ready when I come for you." She leaned in close. "Say nothing. Go along with the preparations for tonight."

Rahab nodded.

Tahirah rose to leave. "If all goes well..."

Rahab stood and embraced her.

"Oh."

"I'm sorry. I know I'm not supposed to..."

"I would want someone to help. If it were me," Tahirah said, patting Rahab's arm. "Promise you'll be safe. It's not going to be easy. I fear this might not work."

"It has to. I can't bear many more days locked away."

"I'll send for the women."

Rahab spent the next several hours being dipped, dabbed, and dressed. She kept to herself and let the experienced hands of the women guide her.

Just before nightfall, Rahab heard a voice at her door, "Mistress, may I enter?"

"Enter."

Tahirah came in carrying a large folded cloth. "Mistress Rahab, you look lovely."

Rahab looked down at the fine silk dress and the brightly-colored gems that covered her.

"This is for you."

Rahab tilted her head.

The maid slowly lifted the top layer of cloth in her hand. She revealed a shimmering, jewel-encrusted necklace. "It's one of Master Ahio's most expensive pieces."

"Don't you think this will draw too much attention?" Rahab spoke low.

"Oh, Mistress, Master Ahio *insisted* you wear this tonight when you are presented."

"Really?" Rahab smiled. She ran her fingers over the polished gems. "It's magnificent. More magnificent than anything I've ever seen, even at the temple."

Tahirah moved Rahab's hair to the side and fastened it around her neck. She leaned in close and whispered, "It'll fetch a large trade too."

Rahab stifled a snort. "It's heavy."

"Most yokes are." Tahirah held up a nearby polished brass mirror.

"I see what you mean."

"Now, you're ready. I will escort you past the guards on our way to the feast hall. To everyone's eyes, we will be making our way to the gathering. When it's time, I will guide you to the servant's quarters. No one is in there because they are all busy serving Master Ahio and his guests. I've got a horse waiting for you. It has some provisions for the trip. Do you know where you'll go?"

"Home. It's all I know."

"Mistress, I strongly urge you to find shelter elsewhere. Jericho is the first place Ahio will come looking for you."

"I can take care of myself. The king is an old customer. If I need it, I can seek his protection. He wouldn't be pushed around by a foreign ambassador."

Echoes of merriment bounced off the long walls as Rahab walked with Tahirah toward the banquet room.

"There sure are a lot of guards," Rahab said, passing another group of heavily armed men.

"I told you. This isn't going to be easy. It's your only chance to taste freedom."

They came close to the servant's chambers.

"Grab your head," Tahirah whispered.

Rahab obeyed.

"Mistress, are you ill?" Tahirah grabbed Rahab's elbow.

"Oh," Rahab moaned.

A guard moved close.

"We'll only be a moment. No need for assistance." She waved him off.

He nodded and stepped back.

"This way, Mistress."

The two entered the servant's chambers.

Tahirah closed the door. "Good. Our time is short...."

"What's going on here?" a voice called.

"I thought you said no one was supposed to be in here," Rahab whispered.

"They weren't." Tahirah pushed Rahab's hand to her head. "Keep it up."

"Mistress Rahab, are you ill?" a servant asked.

"Oh!"

"The Mistress merely needs some fresh air.

She is a bit dizzy from all the excitement."

"I see."

"Would you mind fetching some oil for her?" Tahirah asked. "I think it would do her some good."

"Yes, right away." The servant rushed out the door.

"That was close," Rahab said.

"Yes. She'll be back soon. We need to move."

Tahirah led her out the back door. "Wait here a moment." She tucked behind the building. When she returned, Tahirah led out a packed horse. "He's all ready for you."

"Thank you," Rahab said as she mounted the animal. "I won't forget your kindness."

"Ride quickly. Keep off the main roads if you can."

Tahirah reached back and slapped the horse's hindquarters. "Quick. Go!"

Rahab pushed the horse as far as he would travel until she had to stop.

"Easy there," she said, patting the large horse. "Take a break for now. But we have to move again soon."

Rahab got down and searched through the side bag to find some bread and fresh fruit. She shared some with the horse and rested against him until they both had caught their breath. Rahab stood and surveyed the desert. "It won't be much longer until we reach Jericho. We're very close."

Chapter 8

*"But ye said, 'No; for we will flee upon horses;
therefore shall ye flee:' and, 'We will ride upon
the swift; therefore shall they that pursue you be
swift.' "*
-ISAIAH 30:16

As Rahab rode over a sand dune, the sun began to rise over the large city of Jericho in the distance.

"Home," she said and pointed the horse towards the gates.

She dismounted and led the large animal through the freshly opened gates. They made their way down the open market street.

"It's early, but I'm sure I can find someone to trade with."

Searching the booths, Rahab found a jeweler who was beginning to lay out his products for the busy day ahead.

"Greetings. I have much to trade for you this day," she said, with as much softness as she could manage with a dry throat.

The merchantman looked her over. "Let's see."

Rahab took off all the jewels she had been decorated with and placed them down in front of the man.

He looked through the pile.

"Oh, wait." She took off the large necklace and laid it on top. "This too."

After haggling over a price, Rahab collected her coins and went to the nearest cloth booth.

"How much for this one?" she asked, holding up a simple dress.

Rahab paid for the dress along with a second.

"Just one last thing." She patted the horse. "Sorry. You're a wonderful horse. But you stand out too much. Besides, I don't even know where I'm going to lay my head tonight, much less yours." Rahab buried her head in his thick, black mane.

"Sister?" a voice called behind Rahab. She turned to see Alma and ran towards her.

The two embraced.

"Alma," Rahab cupped her younger sister's cheeks in her hands. "I can't tell you how happy I am to see you." She kissed her cheeks over and over again.

"Sister, what happened to you?" She hugged Rahab again. "I went to the temple to see you. They said you weren't there anymore."

Rahab noticed Alma's eyes start to water.

"They wouldn't tell me what happened to you." She rested her head on Rahab's shoulder. "I was so scared."

"I'm well now." Rahab held her at arm's length. "You know these merchants better than me. Can you help me find someone to buy this big guy?" She reached up to pat the horse.

"Why would you want to sell him? He's gorgeous." Alma rubbed the horse's large nose.

"I'd keep him if I could. But I need the coins more."

"I think I might know a guy."

"Oh, and I need a place to change," Rahab said as she lifted up her silk dress.

"That doesn't look like Temple colors."

"It's not. Let's get this last stuff traded. Then we can find somewhere to talk. I've got a lot to tell you."

A few hours later, Rahab and Alma shared a meal at the city Inn.

"What are you going to do now?"

"I'm not sure. I need to go back to the Temple."

"Rahab, do you really think that's a good idea?"

"Not for work. I've got to talk to Mirit. She'll be able to help me."

"Mirit?" Alma asked. She ripped a piece of flatbread and dipped it in the small bowl of herbs and oil.

"She's an old friend."

"I see. Can I come with you?"

"I don't think so. You need to hurry home. Mother is probably worried sick about you."

"You're right." Alma took another bite of stew from her bowl. "Where are you staying tonight?"

"I'll see if they have a room here."

"Can I come see you?"

"Sure."

After seeing Alma off, Rahab made her way to the Temple of Astarte.

Shuffling through the crowd, she found a familiar face. "Fatima."

"Rahab?" The woman came near. "What are you doing here?"

"I need to find Mirit. Have you seen her?"

"Mirit? You didn't hear?"

"Hear what?"

"Mirit's dead."

"Dead?" Rahab gasped. "What happened to her?"

"I'm not sure. The priests told us she died. They wouldn't let us see her or anything."

Rahab's face grew hot.

"They had me pack up her stuff. I had to turn it all over to them."

"Thank you." Rahab turned away. "I need to speak with them."

"Wait," Fatima pulled Rahab's arm. "There's no talking to them. They're not going to give you any information. Besides, you aren't even supposed to be here. Rumor had it they let you go and you left Jericho."

"That's not the full truth. I was taken by force."

Fatima released her arm. "I know. Mirit told me. She also gave me something."

"What?"

Fatima reached into her pouch and produced a rolled-up parchment. "The night you left, Mirit was terrified. She came back to the room shaking. She told me what happened to you. Gave me this to hide. Said if you ever came back to make sure I got it to you. It seemed pretty important to her."

Rahab took the parchment. "What is it?"

"I didn't look at it. I had almost forgotten about it until I found out Mirit had died. It didn't seem right to turn it in after how she said the priest just let that man take you." She shrugged. "Figured I could get it to you. Eventually."

"Thank you for protecting it."

"What are you going to do now? You know the priests will make you miserable if you come back. Probably make you a slave or something."

Rahab nodded. "You may be right. I've got to figure out what kind of options I have."

"May Astarte bless you, Rahab."

"Thanks," she said as she left the temple.

Astarte is the last being I need help from right now.

Sitting at an empty table in the Inn, Rahab unrolled the parchment. Her eyes searched the document. She sat back and let the paper roll up again.

"Rahab," Alma called, as she entered the dining room of the Inn. "Rahab?"

"Alma, what time is it?"

"The sun is hanging low in the sky. Have you been here all afternoon?"

"Yes. I've been doing a lot of thinking."

Alma sat across from Rahab. "Did you find your friend at the Temple?"

"No. She died."

"Oh, sister. I'm sorry."

"Me too."

"What's this?" Alma said, turning the rolled parchment towards herself.

"That's what I've been thinking about."

Alma unrolled the scroll. "What does it say?"

"It's an agreement between an Inn Keeper and Mirit. She was buying a partnership in exchange for work. It also talks about an agreement to bring in former temple priestesses as harlots to work in the Inn."

"Why?"

"Mirit was getting old. She was already past her required service. The priests would grow weary of her soon. She was doing more training than anything else."

"So why do you have the parchment?"

"It has my name in it."

"Where?" Alma searched the script, but didn't know many of her letters.

Rahab tapped at a spot on the scroll. "Mirit left it for me. Part of the agreement also included a place for me. Even some ownership in the Inn if I wanted."

"That's pretty impressive."

"Yes. I just keep thinking, why me?" Rahab took a sip from her small cup. "I mean, I don't know when she wrote this. If it was before or after I had been taken from Jericho."

"Maybe she knew you'd come back."

"What if I didn't?"

Alma shrugged. "Maybe she was going to buy you back."

A woman walked up to the table. "You want something to eat?"

"Yes, please. Flatbread and some lamb," Alma asked.

"You?"

"That would be fine," Rahab agreed.

"I'll bring some."

"Good," Rahab said. "Also, do you have any rooms for rent tonight?"

"Let me go ask Yaffa. She keeps the rooms."

A few moments later, an ample woman walked toward them. "You asking about a room?"

"Yes," Rahab said. "I am. For tonight. Maybe for a few nights."

"I think I have something available. What are you called?"

"Rahab."

"Where did you get this?" Yaffa picked up the parchment.

"A friend left it for me. I've been trying to figure it out."

"Rahab? Are you from the Temple of Astarte?"

"I was. I no longer belong there."

"Did you know a woman named Mirit there?"

"Yes."

"I haven't seen her in weeks."

"You didn't hear?"

"No. Did something happen?"

"She died."

"How?"

"I don't know. I don't have any more information."

"Such a shame. She was such a wonderful woman."

Rahab nodded. "You knew her well?"

"Well enough. She spent many days here." She pointed to the scroll. "We made this agreement a few months ago. She had this plan." Yaffa smiled. "Mirit knew her time at the temple was growing short. She also knew many former priestesses looking for work. Plenty more who would have to leave the temple and not know what to do with themselves. Her idea was to rent out some of my rooms to those women. Let them earn wages by bringing in male customers. The Inn would make a profit and the women wouldn't have to live on the streets."

"I see."

"Rahab, you're Rahab. She spoke often of you. She had hoped you'd be one of the first to come stay with us."

"Really?"

"Yes. She even made me add in this part about

letting you be a partner with her if you wanted," Yaffa said, pointing to the bottom of the scroll.

"Why?"

Yaffa rolled up the parchment. "She talked about you like a daughter. Cared very deeply for you. Said you came to the temple so young." She lifted Rahab's chin. "Mirit always talked about your honey-colored eyes. I see what she meant. I'm sure you could catch anyone with those."

"Why did you agree to a partnership?" Alma spoke up.

"Seemed like a great plan. I'm not getting any younger. I needed someone I could trust to assist me. With Mirit's help and more income, I could slow down a little. Not have to work so hard all the time."

"Mirit's plan does sound good," Alma agreed.

"What do you say, Honey?"

"Excuse me?"

Yaffa waved the rolled-up parchment around. "You in?"

"Oh, Rahab. Do it."

"I don't know."

"It would mean a roof over your head. And you wouldn't have to go back to the Temple. Or worse."

"I'll offer you the same bargain," Yaffa said. "Partner? You supply the girls. I supply the Inn. We take some of the profit they make, plus room and board. I'll even set you up in a room so you can have customers too."

Rahab looked at the wide eyes of her sister.

"You should," she beamed.

"Alright. I'll become your partner."

"Great."

The servant woman returned with a plate of lamb and bread.

"I'll cover your meal and room tonight. You start work tomorrow bringing us some girls."

Chapter 9

*"Likewise, I say unto you, there is joy in the
presence of the angels of God over one sinner
that repenteth."*
-LUKE 15:10

"Every time I hear a story about those desert
people, it makes me laugh."

"Yes, my king." She had heard all the same
stories before, but the king always made them
sound even more impressive. It was also his
favorite thing to talk about.

She didn't mind his talk or his money.

Rahab had settled in at the Inn. She gained a
growing client list with many high paying officials.
She had opened rooms up to former priestesses
who worked as city women. Mirit's plan had
worked well and much in Rahab's favor.

The king rolled over to his back. "Though
nothing makes me smile more than you, Rahab.
Not even the tales of those silly wanderers."

Rahab heard his breathing change and she
knew what would come next.

"Why don't you leave this place." He waved

around the room. "Come live in the palace. I could have you anytime I wanted, and you could have everything you ever wanted."

It was not the first time he had made the offer and Rahab was sure it would not be the last.

To any other harlot, an invitation to live in the palace and be the king's royal concubine would be a dream come true, but not for Rahab. She finally had what she always wanted, freedom and control. Choices; she finally had choices.

"No. Thank you. I am quite happy here," she said, rising to her feet.

"I don't see how," the king glanced around the room.

Rahab helped the king get dressed and saw him out the door.

As the king left with his guards, one of them turned back to Rahab before she could close the door. He pressed it open with his large hand and put his face down to Rahab's level.

"You got some left for me?" He smiled wide.

"No."

"Aw. Come now, harlot. I'm not good enough for you?"

Rahab pushed on the door without success. "You could not afford me," she stabbed.

"You're probably not as good as they say you are anyway." The guard huffed.

"You will never find out."

He let his hand off the door and stepped back. "You think you're so smart. The law may forbid me to enter without permission, harlot, but just remember who enforces the laws around here. One night, I might just wipe that smug smile off your pretty, little face."

Rahab quickly slammed the door shut.

She sat down and leaned her back against the door. Listening to the loud footsteps fade away, Rahab took a deep breath to regain herself.

She stood and moved across the room to count her earnings for the night. It was still too early to stop for the night, but Rahab's body grew tired. It screamed for attention and Rahab was powerless to fight it. She made her way over to the soft wool blankets before she passed out.

A knock at Rahab's door woke her from another dark sleep. She had spent years working and helping to run the Inn, but it didn't help the dreams that haunted her each night she laid her head down.

She made her way toward the sound and opened the door expecting to see a well-dressed man standing there with a money bag outstretched. Shielding her eyes from the early rising sun, Rahab blinked enough to make out the figure. She rolled her eyes.

"What is it, Alma?" she croaked.

The smiling face of her youngest sister told her

the answer before she had to ask. "Greetings, Rahab. Can I spend the day with you?"

Rahab leaned against the wooden door. "Why would you want to do that?"

Alma chuckled. "Oh, Sister. You know how much I enjoy being with you." She pushed the door open enough to slide her small frame inside.

"Sure, why don't you come on in," Rahab said.

Alma squealed.

Rahab winced at the sound. It reminded her so much of her brother Noda. She had been dreaming about him again. Rahab rubbed her forehead at the unwanted memories.

"Please, sit." Rahab waved to a pile of clean blankets.

Alma made herself comfortable. "So, what are we going to do today?"

Rahab plopped her body down on her bed. "Sleep," she said as she curled up and closed her eyes.

A push to her shoulder jarred Rahab. "Sister, you are so fun. Really, what are we going to do?"

Rahab rolled over onto her back to stare up at the ceiling. "Well, I do have some flax drying on the roof. I had an idea in mind for it and I could use some help."

Another squeal from her sister's lips made Rahab consider retracting her offer.

Alma clapped her hands and headed out the door.

Rahab sluggishly followed her sister.

When she reached the last step, Rahab saw Alma bent over the long stems.

She stroked them gently. "Yes. They are nice and dry."

"Good."

"So, are you going to make a new dress?" Alma wondered.

"No."

"I know, a new veil."

"No," Rahab said, as she picked up a stalk and began to split it open.

"A new blanket?" Alma said, as she lifted a stalk and copied her sister's motions.

"No."

"I give up. What are you going to do with it?"

Rahab pulled at the satin strains. "A new cord."

Alma gasped. "I always wanted to learn how to do that."

Rahab rolled her eyes at the simple excitement she had brought the young woman.

"It will take some time. I could use some strong help." Rahab looked at her sister out of the corner of her eye.

Arms flew around Rahab.

"Thank you, thank you, thank you. I will do whatever you say. I promise I will be a big help," Alma rambled.

"Sure. Here," she said, as she handed Alma another stalk. "Just like this." Rahab pulled all the strands out of the stalk husk and laid them in one pile and placed the empty stalk in another pile.

"We have to do all of these stalks before we move on to the next step."

Alma's hands went to work pulling at the delicate pieces.

After all the stalks had been broken and cleaned, Rahab showed Alma how to twist the individual strands together to start building the base for the rope.

"You must be vigilant in this process. It is better to take your time and make sure this part is right. Otherwise, when you get it all put together, your rope will not be strong and it will break," she explained as she carefully wound the fibers in her fingers.

Alma imitated her sister's movements.

The two women worked in silence for some time. Until Rahab noticed Alma fidgeting.

"Something wrong? Because if this is too boring, I could find some work for you to do downstairs in the kitchen."

"No, it's not that."

"What is it?"

"May I speak freely?"

"Of course, Sister. You know that."

"Are you coming to the ritual tomorrow?"

There it is.

"No," Rahab answered.

"Come on, sister. You have to go. It is important to our family."

You have no idea.

Alma stared at her sister, waiting for an

explanation.

"I'm not welcomed there."

"That's not true," she huffed. "I am inviting you and that makes you welcome. What's the issue?"

The issue, little sister, is not as simple as an invitation. It's that I am no longer seen as part of your family. You are just too young to understand.

"I'm busy," she lied.

"You are not," Alma fought back.

Rahab looked into the stern eyes of her sister.

She looks just like Noda when he wouldn't get his way.

Rahab choked on the lump in her throat. "Fine, I'm not busy. I just don't want to go."

Alma broke her stare and looked down at the strand in her hand. "Please?" she softened.

"Okay, I'll go," Rahab said.

For you, sister.

Alma leapt up to hug Rahab. "Thank you." She sat and picked up the strand she had been working on. "So, what is the next step?"

Rahab looked around to see all the fibers had been worked into piles of long strands. "Now comes the hard part." Rahab picked up a line and held it up to Alma. "Hold this one," she said as she picked up another and began to work the two together. "We must put all of these strands together into three long sections and then we will twist the sections together to make one long cord. I need you to hold on to this while I work away from it."

Alma nodded as she held onto the strand Rahab began to work on.

"Good girl."

The two worked together until the sun went down. The simple fibers turned into a strong three-fold cord in their hands.

Rahab held the rope up to show Alma their hard work. "See," she said as she pulled at the cord. "Strong."

Alma smiled. "I can see why you needed help."

"Yes, it makes the work so much easier and faster."

"Are we done now?" Alma looked at the empty places surrounding them.

"You are done, but the cord has a few more steps before I am done with it."

Alma tilted her head.

Rahab pulled at the rope again. "I have decided to dye it. I'm going to use it to tie back some curtains downstairs in my room and I want to dye it to match them."

A smile danced across Alma's face. "What a nice idea, Sister. I think it will look beautiful."

"Let me walk you out," she said as she put the cord down and stood up.

The younger woman followed her down the steps. "Are you getting more flax?"

"Yes. I should be getting some more tomorrow. This year has produced a large harvest."

"Thank Astarte."

Yes, let's all thank Astarte. She has done so much for us.

Standing at the open door, Alma turned to her sister. "It was nice to be with you today," she said before she hugged Rahab around the neck.

"You too, Sister."

As the sun set in the western sky, Rahab waited for a knock to come at her door. She didn't have to wait long.

"Enter."

The wooden door swung open to reveal her first client for the night.

"My king," she said, with a deep bow. "It will be my pleasure to serve you this night."

"Very well."

"Make yourself comfortable," she waved to her bed.

An hour later, Rahab watched as the king's breath grew heavy next to her.

"Something you wish to talk about, my king?"

"Hmmm."

She recognized a man who had many thoughts weighing him down.

"My heart is troubled. I fear for the safety of Jericho," the king explained.

Rahab leaned her back against the wall and listened.

"I have kept a careful ear on the stories about the group which walks the desert sand."

The Wanderers.

"At first," the king said looking up, "I did not give them much concern. They seemed..."

"Strange," Rahab finished his thought.

"Yes," he said, glancing over at her. "Still, I kept listening so I would know if they ever became a threat to my city." He paused, holding his breath.

"Have they?" she asked.

The king let out a deep sigh. "I'm afraid they are fast becoming one."

Rahab waited.

"I received word about a month ago. They have destroyed two nearby cities," he blurted.

"Destroyed?" she said, tilting her head.

"Their numbers are great and their mighty men even greater. They came against Heshbon and Bashon with such force that they left nothing untouched in their path. Even going so far as to slaughter Og and Sihon, the cities' respective kings, and murdering every living thing in the towns." Running his finger over the blanket, he groaned, "I fear for the people of my city."

She sat up on her elbows beside him. "Jericho has been built to withstand any army. Our walls are great and our warriors are greater. No one can come against us."

He smiled up at her. "You're right. I have nothing to fear. Especially from a bunch of aimless sons of slaves." Having dressed, the king left the Inn.

After a long night of customers, Rahab tossed

and turned. Visions of Wanders following their cloud and fire danced in her head.

Unable to sleep, she climbed the stairs to her rooftop to stare at the star-filled sky. All the stories of the Wanderers came flooding back to her memory and she felt a deep ache in her soul.

"If you can lead a group of city-less people safely through the desert and then allow them victory over strongly held towns, you have more power than any god or goddess I've ever known." She looked down. "Though, I don't know if that is due to their lack of power or my lot in life." Gazing back up at the vast speckled darkness, she continued, "Regardless, I believe You to be the true God. I know I don't deserve your blessing, and I'm not asking for it. I only acknowledge who You are." Rahab closed her eyes and allowed a cool breeze which washed over her to be her answer.

Chapter 10

*"She seeketh wool, and flax, and worketh
willingly with her hands."*
-PROVERBS 31:13

Covered from head to toe, Rahab moved through
the crowded streets of Jericho with such ease and
comfort her sandaled feet almost floated along the
path toward the ritual gathering across town. Her
head and most of her face were covered by a thick
red veil. Her honey eyes shielded with a sheer
white linen placed perfectly under the veil. If
anyone wanted to look upon her, it would cost
them a handsome sum.

Without a word to anyone, and no word to her
in return, Rahab reached her destination.

The ceremony had already begun by the time
she reached the temple. She was careful to avoid
running into any member of her family.

A voice echoed off the stone walls as Rahab
found a spot in the crowd to watch.

Noticing the red veil, many people stepped
aside to allow her to pass.

Out of the corner of her eye, she saw a man

elbow the man next to him and then point to her.

"There is the harlot everyone talks about."

"The one who can make you...you know...just by looking into her eyes?" The other questioned.

The first man nodded vigorously. "That's what they say."

Shifting his weight to one leg in order to lean in, the second man asked, "Have you ever...you know?"

"With her?" The first man choked.

"Yes."

Rubbing his hand on the back of his neck, the first man answered, "No, never had enough money to waste on her."

"Sure bet it's worth it," the second man said, glaring at Rahab.

Idiots.

Rahab's eyes landed on the dark, hooded figures at the front of the crowd who commanded everyone's attention.

One carried a torch and repeated a prayer while he walked. Another man led a group of small children behind him, some of them were barely able to walk on their own. The one with the torch stopped near the altar and lit the waiting fuel and wood.

Flames raced toward the sky as all eyes watched the fire grow.

The first hooded figure turned around to wave the first child over to himself.

The little boy waddled the few steps toward

the man and smiled up at him.

His trusting eyes grabbed at Rahab's heart, but she pushed aside her feelings and turned her gaze back to the flame.

As the fire grew hotter and brighter, the larger hooded figure continued on with his petitions. With a slight pause, the man reached down for the waiting child and cradled the little one in his arms. Resting a large hand on the small boy's forehead, the man spoke again in his commanding voice as he turned toward the fire. With all eyes on him, the priest lifted the boy high into the air and spoke the last of his prayer before tossing the boy into the flames.

One ear-piercing squeal escaped the boy's mouth before he was engulfed by the fire.

The sound sent a shiver down Rahab's back as she closed her eyes. The smell of burning flesh and the rush of memories from her childhood.

Noda.

Rahab's eyes popped open at the sound of the next child screaming from inside the fire.

The two boy's flesh mingled together, while the screams died down within the flames.

She watched the last child be added to the altar fire, while she grew numb to the sight and choking smell of burnt flesh.

Allowing the children to burn down to the bones, the hooded figures continued their prayers until the moment they extinguished the fire with a large clay pot of sand. They carefully collected the burnt bones in a wide strip of linen.

Leading the way, the two men walked away from the crowd. Offering to the people, without words, to follow them to the next step or leave and continue their day.

Some walked along with the hooded figures, while the rest disbursed to go about their way.

Rahab followed the crowd heading toward the middle of the city and down into the burial chamber.

Finding a place deep enough in the crowd not to draw attention to herself, Rahab watched the hooded figures walk into the chamber.

They stepped up to a stone table encircled by a pit. Placing the extensive collection of bones on top of the table, the two found the three small skulls and set them aside. Gathering all the other bones, the larger of the two men began to pray aloud again as the other deposited the bones into the pile which surrounded the stone table in the pit.

After they finished placing the children's bones on top of the pile, the smaller hooded man reached for a stone bowl and poured a thick, white liquid over the small skulls. Allowing the liquid to harden on the skulls for a few moments, the two men went to work painting decorations on each of the faces.

Once they were done, they each took one skull at a time and placed them into the cut shelves of the rock around the room. The small skulls took their place among those previously sacrificed and would be there when someone needed their help.

A few more prayers were spoken before everyone was dismissed.

As soon as the chamber cleared of mostly everyone, Rahab made her way to the eastern wall. Her eyes fell on the smile-painted face of a small skull. She looked over her shoulder to see others, drawn to individual skulls, were deep in prayer. Rahab turned her attention back to the one in front of her and placed her hands on either side of its cheekbones. Lowering herself to the ground, Rahab stared into the large holes where her brother's eyes once looked out at her.

"I miss you," she whispered. She touched her forehead to her brother's.

The skull did not respond.

"I wish they would have taken me instead of you." She brushed its cheeks with her thumbs. A tear slid down her face. Burying her face in her shoulder, Rahab wiped it away. "I wasn't pure enough for them," she mumbled to herself, looking down at the ledge which held the skull, and then back up at her brother's painted face. She patted the top of his head a few times and then stood. "Help me, brother. If you can hear me... help."

Turning her back on the row of skulls, Rahab climbed the steps into the sun and made her way back to the Inn.

Closing the door to her room, Rahab removed

her red veil so she could take off the sheer fabric which covered her eyes. She only wore it when she went outside.

Replacing the veil on her head, she returned to her work which had been interrupted by the day's ritual. She headed up the stairs to the rooftop where she had left a large pot boiling over a small fire. Rahab picked up the cord Alma had helped her make the day before. She walked to the pot and leaned over to see the liquid had turned a deep crimson red.

Perfect.

Lowering the material down into the warm liquid, Rahab grabbed the large stick which lay nearby and stirred the cord so it would be completely coated in the dye. While it cooked, she sat down to watch the bubbles boil away in the water. She was mesmerized at how similar the liquid looked to the burning flesh and blood of children in the altar fire.

The screams of her younger brother erupted in her memory.

She shook her head to clear the thoughts.

Though there was much more to be done, Rahab's body cried out to remain still. Closing her eyes, she allowed rest to cradle her body as she leaned up against part of the short, stone wall of the roof.

The brief quietness was once again interrupted with screams from her memory. Only these screams came not from her brother's mouth, but from her own. The red color of the boiling liquid drew the horrific events of her childhood out of her hidden past and displayed them afresh to relive the pain all over again.

She woke with a jolt.

Sleep only brings dreams. Dreams only bring back the nightmares.

Soon, the sound of knocking would be heard at Rahab's door. Men would rotate in and out of her room for hours.

After cleaning up, Rahab's body ached. She knew she needed sleep if she were going to be any good later. Pure exhaustion had become the only way she knew to convince her body to sleep lately. It was not just her profession which kept her awake at night and working hard all day, but her tormented past haunted her like a restless soul haunted the earth.

When she stirred, the sun had gone down and the air around her had grown colder. Rahab went up to her rooftop to fix a pot of her special tea she used to relax her customers. She looked out over the short wall to see the people of Jericho hide themselves away behind closed doors.

As she crushed the herbs into a fine powder, Rahab realized the fire had died out and she remembered the cord. Grabbing the stick, she lifted the rope out of the colored water and laid it on the stain colored part of her roof she had set aside for drying her dyed garments. Being careful to remove the pot and set the dye aside, Rahab stirred the fire and set a small pot of water over it.

Just before the water got hot enough to boil, she poured some of the water into the clay vessel where she had placed the ground herbs.

Some men seemed to need more help relaxing and her unique blend put them right at ease. At the same time, it kept anyone from overpowering her.

From where she sat, Rahab could see far out into the city of Jericho. When the sun fell behind the mountains and the moon shone bright in the night sky, a different sort of person would roam the streets. During the day, the families would wander about with their daily activities; people smiled and children played. While during the night, people searched for trouble or drank their problems away. Some would visit Rahab, or others like her, to enjoy an hour or so getting the pleasure they paid for.

She took the tea with her down the stairs and back to her room. Her first customer would arrive at any moment.

Rahab spent the next day showing her sister more weaving techniques and even began to show Alma which things she used to make her liquid mixes for different colors to dye the fabrics and cords.

As they sat working together on the roof, Alma

looked up. The sun which had made its journey across the sky for the day. "I guess I should get going. It's late and I don't want to be in the way of your clients tonight." She stood.

"You don't need to go. If you don't want to," Rahab said, as she kept running her needle through the material in her hand.

"Won't you be expecting your first visitor soon? The sun is almost set." She pointed to the large light growing dim in the sky.

Rahab shook her head. "Not tonight."

Alma knelt beside her older sister. "I don't understand."

"I think I am going to give up being a harlot. Or, at the very least, cut back how many nights I entertain clients. With Yaffa gone, it's getting to be a lot of work to run the Inn and entertain clients." She held up the dress in her hands to check her progress.

"Will running the Inn alone be enough?"

Satisfied, Rahab picked up the place she had stopped. "I have been meaning to talk to you about that."

"Me?"

Rahab looked around, "Is there anyone else on this rooftop?"

Alma looked around to be sure.

The motion set Rahab into a fit of laughter. "Oh, Sister. I think I'm getting pretty good at creating garments," she said, as she held up the dress in her hands for her sister to examine.

"You make the best garments I've ever seen." Alma picked up the hem of her dress as evidence.

Rahab rolled her eyes. "Anyway, I have enough money stored. The Inn is doing well. Lots of women have come to work for me here. I think I have a plan for something else."

"Plan?"

"Yes. The truth is, no one wants to buy things from a harlot. I was thinking. No one would have a problem buying from you."

"Me?" Alma pointed to her chest.

"Yes, you." Rahab sighed. "Sister, you are innocently sweet. Yet, I've seen you haggle in the market. If we pass off the clothes I make as coming from your hand, people will line up to pay for them. I'll split the profit with you if you take the garments to the market, sell them, and maybe help out with cleaning the flax and such."

Alma stared blankly. "You're serious."

"I am," she smiled and continued sewing.

Alma hugged her sister. "I'm so proud of you."

"What?"

She hugged her again. "For wishing to do honorable work."

"I just don't know if I want to sell my body anymore. I'm not getting any younger."

Her sister hesitated for a moment.

"What is it?" Rahab asked concerned. "Do you not agree with the plan?"

"No. It's not that," she said, leaning back on her heels. "I think there is more than you are telling me."

Rahab took a deep breath. "I think I need a change and this seems like a pretty good idea to me."

"Yes, it is a good plan. But you know you can tell me anything."

"I know." Rahab looked up at the dark sky. "You must be hungry. How about some stew?"

Alma squealed with delight. "I'll get some from the kitchen."

Chapter 11

"And Joshua the son of Nun sent out of Shittim two men to spy secretly, saying, 'Go view the land, even Jericho.' And they went, and came into an harlot's house, named Rahab, and lodged there."
-JOSHUA 2:1

Rahab arranged some freshly cut flax stalks out on her rooftop. She wiped some beads of sweat off her brow and found the sun hanging low in the sky. Adjusting the last stalk, she sat on the edge of the wall to look out onto the city.

Her gaze drifted over the people moving through the streets until it fell on two men. Rahab's heart began to race.

"Visitors," she told herself. "Jericho gets dozens every day."

But something is different.

She watched them as they watched the people carefully. Too carefully for Rahab's comfort.

They eyed the walls as if they were made of gold and studied their surroundings.

Her breath quickened as they turned down the

street toward her Inn.

She rushed down the stairs and into the dining room.

The two men had just come into the room and had sat at an empty table.

She hid in the archway for a moment to study them.

The first looked older. He had a dark black beard to match his curly hair, but both had been painted with gray. His muscles were sturdy for a man of advanced age. His features were hard, as if he had spent his whole life out in the sun and wind of the desert. A large nose and almond-shaped eyes seemed out of place in the crowd of softer faces in the room.

They were surely not from Jericho.

The second man seemed younger in the smoothness of his face, yet his build was that of a warrior.

Rahab's heart began to pound harder as she stared into the topaz eyes of the tall stranger. She tried to control her breath by looking away and finding something else to stare at, but her gaze kept returning to the strangers.

Straightening her veil, Rahab walked over to one of her Inn workers. "Have they ordered yet?" She motioned to the men.

"Yes. They were also asking about a room."

"Let me handle it."

Rahab walked to the table. "I heard you guys were looking for a room?"

"Yes. Do you have one?"

"For the night or something shorter?" Rahab asked.

"We are not here for that," the older man said.

Rahab tilted her head to the side and narrowed her eyes. "You guys lost?"

She heard the taller man swallow hard.

"No, ma'am. We just need a place to spend the night."

"Yes, we don't need your...*services*," the older sneered.

"I don't know if I have any rooms." Rahab shifted her weight to one leg. "There is another Inn not too far from here. I could show you the way..."

"Protect my men, Rahab," a voice called so close it made her turn around.

No one was there.

"If it is all the same to you," the taller man said, getting her attention. "I think we would be more comfortable here."

She thought for a moment. "I don't have any rooms available for only overnight guests."

"Rahab!" The odd voice screamed, "Protect my men."

Turning herself around in a circle, she searched for the person who yelled at her.

The two men exchanged a quick glance.

The older shrugged his shoulders.

"Are you alright?" the younger man asked.

"Fine," she said, more to the voice than the

men. "I will make some arrangements. But the fee is going to be high."

"Rahab," the voice said.

She tapped her foot a few times. "Forget the fee. Don't tell anyone and I'll put you up for the night. One night."

"Promise," the tall one agreed.

"What are you called?"

"Caleb," the older said, over a mouthful of stew.

"I'm called Salmon," the tall one said.

"You can call me Rahab. When you are done eating, let the woman know and I'll show you to your room."

She walked over to her servant girl.

"We don't have any open rooms."

"I know," Rahab said. "I'm going to put them up in my room for the night."

"Here we are," Rahab said, opening the door.

The men sat down in Rahab's room and began to discuss their plans in hushed tones.

Rahab paced around the room.

A few moments later, pounding came at the door.

"Rahab, I think you'd better get downstairs," a servant called. "The king's men are in the dining room asking for the two strangers."

"Send them away."

"I've tried. They are refusing to leave."

"Try harder."

Heavy footsteps rushed down the hall.

"We know you have those spies, Rahab," a husky voice called. "Give them over and you will not be harmed."

Rahab held her tongue and waved for the strangers to follow her out the side door and up the stairs.

Once they reached the rooftop, she pulled up some flax stalks which were laid out to dry. Leaning over to Caleb, she whispered, "Get underneath and don't breathe a word."

She waited until both of the large men were under the long stalks before covering them.

Rahab rushed back down the stairs before the king's men could break in her door. She reached the door and ripped it open just in time. "May I help you?" Rahab asked, as she tried to calm her panting breaths.

"Hand over the spies," the leader demanded.

"Spies?" Rahab played innocent. "There are no spies here."

A short man pushed to the front. "Witnesses said they came into this Inn. Now, bring them out so we can take them to the king."

Rahab dipped her head and pretended to think for a minute. "Hmm, spies you say?"

"Yes, two of them," the larger man snorted.

"Well, two men did come by here earlier.

They ordered some food, but they left right before it got dark. I believe they headed out of the gates just before they were shut up for the night. If they were spies, you should run after them. You might be able to catch up to them. Go, hurry," she said, as she pushed the biggest man.

"Come, men." The leader drew his sword high in the air and charged down the stairs.

As the others followed after him, Rahab closed the door and pressed her back against it for a moment. She had never laid on a lie so thick before, but she had never felt such peace before.

"Well done," the voice whispered.

She jumped and looked around the large room.

"W-W-Who's there?" she called.

No answer.

Shaking off the fear she was losing her senses, Rahab pressed her ear up to the large wooden door. She had to make sure the footsteps were still moving away. Hearing no noise, Rahab climbed the stairs to her rooftop.

Kneeling down, she carefully lifted a few pieces of flax off the pile to uncover the first spy. Her veiled eyes met those of Salmon and, for a moment, she paused. Gazing into eyes of pure topaz unlike any she had seen before, Rahab's heart skipped a beat and she suddenly had trouble breathing.

"Are they gone?" Salmon asked, after a few moments of held breath.

"Y-y-yes." Rahab trembled. She swallowed

hard and continued to remove the flax from his body.

When she had him clear enough, she moved to the next pile to uncover Caleb.

Rahab led the two men back down the stairs.

Once inside, she picked up a bowl of grains and fish that had been delivered to her room by one of her girls. Rahab studied each man. A deep fear grew insider her. "You guys are not from Jericho, are you?" she wondered aloud.

The men shared a quick glance.

Rahab looked down at her uneaten food and sighed deeply. She closed her eyes and listened for something to tell her what to do with the two men who sat before her.

"I know your God has given you our land," Rahab broke the heavy silence.

The two men turned their heads toward each other and then back to Rahab.

"You are Wanderers, are you not?" she said, still staring into her own bowl.

The two men did not know if they should answer.

Rahab lifted her head slightly. "I've heard stories of your powerful God."

"How do you know of our God?" Caleb questioned.

She took a deep breath. "We have heard of all the plagues and how the Lord dried up the water of the Red sea for you, when you came out of Egypt, and what He did unto the two kings of the

Amorites who were on the other side of the Jordan." Rahab looked out the window across the room. "When we heard all these things, our hearts melted and we became very afraid because your terror has fallen on us. The Lord, your God, He is in heaven above and in earth below." She looked back down at her feet.

Caleb looked over at Salmon, who was staring wide-mouthed at Rahab.

"You are right when you say our God is strong. We believe he has given this land to us and will help us take it." Salmon said.

Rahab nodded. "I believe that as well." She put her bowl down and gathered her knees to her chest. "I know our walls are strong, built by cunning men with the best materials, but I believe your God to be stronger," she said as she fought back the tears which burned her eyes.

"Those who build the strongest walls have the most to hide," Salmon said.

Rahab paused and thought on the idea. She had built many walls herself. Though not with her hands, but by her actions.

Alma's young face flashed in her mind. Fighting back tears, she locked eyes with Salmon and pleaded, "Please, I beg you, swear to me by the Lord, since I have shown you such kindness, that you show kindness unto my family and give me a sign of your word."

"Our life for yours," Salmon answered.

"What?" Caleb interrupted.

Salmon looked over at his friend. "She did spare our lives. If it were not for her kindness, our heads would be rolling around the tiled floor of the palace by now."

Caleb huffed. "On one condition, then."

"Name it." Rahab breathed.

"On the condition, you do not speak our business to any," Caleb clarified.

Rahab bowed her head. "Agreed."

Salmon continued, "Then it shall be when the Lord has given us this land, we will deal kindly and truly with you and your family."

"Thank you," Rahab fought the tears which blinded her sight. Knowing the two men could not see them past the sheer veil even if they were to spill over; she pressed her sleeve against her face so the material would soak up the moisture. Satisfied they did not notice the motion, she turned back to her bowl of food and indulged her raging stomach while to two men talked.

Hours later, Rahab caught Salmon nodding his head quickly a few times.

Caleb turned toward her. "We need to get out of here. Do you know a way of escape? Those guards won't be long looking for us before they realize you had not spoken truth," Caleb said, as he stood.

Rahab thought for a moment about sneaking them out of the city. *It's night and no one would see them, but it's too risky. He's right, the guards would be back soon and the two men were no match for a strong army.*

"Come," she said, putting down the dress she was sewing. She led them to her large window which looked out over the desert.

Salmon stood behind her. "This house is built into the wall?"

Rahab looked up at him over her shoulder.

He was looking up at the ceiling, but shifted his gaze to her just as she turned her face back out the window.

Looking down, she tried to guess how far it was to the sand below. Jumping would cause too much of an injury to either man. She spun around to face Salmon's broad chest. Blushing, for the first time since she could remember, Rahab moved past him and glanced around the room. Nothing large enough for her to lower the men in.

Think!

As her eyes glanced around the room once again, she saw the long crimson cord tied around her curtains.

That just might work.

Stepping quickly, she untied it and made her way back to Salmon. Without asking, she wrapped the cord around him and tied a careful knot at his waist.

His wide-eyed look made her hesitate for a

moment.

"I can lower you down. It is the safest way to get you out of Jericho," she said, holding the other end of the rope

"Are you crazy?" Caleb said, clearing the room to stand at Salmon's side.

Salmon looked down at Rahab.

"Trust me?" She looked up with pleading eyes.

"With my life," he nodded and then stepped onto the window ledge.

She moved closer toward him and he reached for her hand. "Take this cord and tie it in this window," he patted the ledge, "gather your family together in this house and do not allow any to leave. Any who are outside of your home when we return, their blood will be spilled and we shall be blameless of it. When we come into the land, we will see the cord and spare the lives of all inside, but only inside. Do you understand?"

"Thank you," she said as she began to let him down.

"Easy. Here, let me help," Caleb said. He grabbed the middle of the cord. "Slow."

Salmon nodded and then slid both of his feet out of the window. Turning around, he clutched the edge before carefully easing his weight onto the rope.

The two on the other end slowly let out the slack until they felt the rope tension ease.

"I'm on the ground," Salmon called up.

They waited a moment before pulling the cord

back through the window.

Caleb tied the loose end around his waist and then sat on the ledge throwing his feet over the edge. He looked down at Salmon before turning back to Rahab.

"Head toward the mountains," she insisted. "The king's men will still be searching for you, so do not head straight to your camp. Lay low in the mountain for a few days and then you may return to your people."

Caleb looked down at the ground again. "If you betray us..." he warned, as he turned to look her in the eyes, "...we will be blameless of your blood."

Rahab nodded a few times and let him down. When she felt the rope give, she leaned over to see the two men standing in the sand.

Caleb looked up as Salmon helped untie him and called to her, "Remember, tell no one or your blood shall mix with the others on the streets of Jericho."

"According to your words, so be it. Go now," she said and secured the crimson cord to the window.

She watched them flee toward the distant mountains until she could no longer make out their shapes against the sand.

Rahab sat down with her back pressed against the wall. She felt tears growing in her eyes and, for the first time since she was a little girl, she let them flow freely. Crying herself to sleep, she thought on

Salmon's face and slept for the first time in years without a single nightmare.

Chapter 12

"Behold, I send an Angel before thee, to keep thee in the way, and to bring thee into the place which I have prepared."
-EXODUS 23:20

The rays of sunlight danced across Rahab's face until she began to stir. Rolling over on the hard floor, she blinked her eyes a few times before looking around. Meeting the two men last night had done something to her.

Rising slowly, Rahab lifted herself up to look out her window. The crimson cord blew in the wind as she gazed out over the desert.

Somewhere in the mountains, she hoped the two spies were hiding.

Rahab trusted they would stay there for a few days before heading back to their camp to share their report with their leader. There was time to prepare, but not much. Soon the army of the Wanderers would be marching on her city and she would need to be ready.

Turning around to face her cleaning area, Rahab slowly made her way over to the water bowl. Before this day, she hardly spent time looking into her reflection beyond making sure her eye and lip color were applied correctly. In that moment, she felt drawn to look at her face. She could feel a change on the inside and wanted to see if there was a difference on the outside as well. Leaning cautiously over the edge of the large bowl she slowly opened her eyes to see herself staring back. There was no physical change in her appearance, though there was something different she could not quite put her finger on.

Her eyes shined a little brighter and she was smiling. Reaching her hands up to her face, she touched her lips and cheeks. Yes, she was smiling. Rahab had not smiled much. Well, not a genuine smile anyway. She had painted a smile on her face to put nervous men at ease, but an unprovoked one like what she was wearing now had not been there in a long time.

Feeling her own face made it real, but she still could not wrap her mind around it. She sat down on the floor and looked out the window.

"Thank you, God of the Israelites," she said. "I do believe you to be the one, true God."

Just then, a flash of brilliant light forced Rahab to close her eyes and throw her arms over her face. At first, she thought the sun had moved enough to fully shine in her window, but it was too early for that to be true. Barely managing to open her eyes against the light, Rahab could make out a towering figure who had suddenly appeared in her room.

Her knees hit the stone floor hard and she laid her forehead to the ground.

"Spare my life," she cried as she covered her head with her hands.

"Peace, Rahab. I am called Gabriel and I come with a message from God," his voice rumbled. "You have done well to protect the children of God and your life will be spared in return. God wants you to see that you carry a heavy responsibility on your shoulders. You must not tell anyone what you spoke of with the spies and you must not tell them what I will show you."

"It will be done as you have spoken." Rahab trembled.

"Rise then and go to the window," he commanded.

Slowly, Rahab picked herself up and shielded her eyes from the radiant being standing before her. Squinting, she could make out only some of his features.

The man, if a man, was very tall. So tall, that his head touched the ceiling and probably would have passed through it if he were he any taller. His body radiated pure light which washed out everything else in the room and wrapped around Rahab like a tight covering. He had wings coming out of his back, but they did not look like the wings of a bird. They were more like two shields attached to his body. Yet they flapped up and down like birds' wings.

She could not make out his face or much of

anything else, other than he was pointing toward her window. Walking around his tree-trunk legs, she made her way to the window and peered outside. The sight she saw made her gasp.

Holding her eyes wide open, Rahab looked out on the desert to see a massive army of soldiers who looked very similar to the being which stood in her room. The striking difference was the army was dressed in full battle armor which shone bright in the rising sun. The one who stood in the room with her dressed only in a white robe with a belt tied around his waist.

"Who are they?" She stared, daring not to blink.

"The host of God."

The countless beings filled the desert in front of Rahab's window as far as she could see. They stood with swords drawn and eyes focused on the walls of Jericho.

"They look like they are prepared for battle."

"They are."

There was a long pause while Rahab's eyes flowed over the crowd.

"The one in front there is Michael," Gabriel said as Rahab's eyes landed on the great being standing a few steps in front of the others.

When Rahab finally blinked, the beings disappeared and all that was left was the sand staring back at her. She spun around to face Gabriel. "Where did they go?"

Gabriel chuckled, his voice tingling in some

strange melody. "They are still there. God lifted the veil from your eyes for a few moments so you could see the army which waits to destroy the evil in this city."

Rahab thought for a moment. "I thought the army of Israel was coming to conquer Jericho."

"Jericho will fall, but not at the hands of the Israelites. There is more for you to see. Go to the door."

Walking around Gabriel's massive legs once more, Rahab made her way downstairs to the front door.

The Inn dining room was empty and would not open for hours.

"Open it and look on the streets of Jericho."

Cautiously, she opened the door and peered outside. A scream escaped from her mouth as she slammed the door shut. She pressed her body hard against the wood. Her body trembled and her eyes burned with tears.

"Peace," Gabriel said. "They cannot harm you."

Rahab huddled against the door. The vision of the horrible creatures who climbed inside the men the night she was defiled came flooding back to her.

"Open it," Gabriel's voice called. "They cannot harm you."

Rahab took a deep breath and opened the door enough to peek out into the streets. She could see thousands of ugly beings torturing the people of

Jericho. She took a few shallow breaths and allowed the light from Gabriel to wrap around her again before she spoke, "Who are they?"

"Fallen ones."

"I've seen ones like their kind before," she closed her eyes and pressed her cheek hard against the door.

"Peace."

She turned her back to the door and looked up at Gabriel. "They hurt me before."

"I know." His voice was soft. "God allows humans to endure things they cannot understand so His plan may be fulfilled in ways none of us could comprehend. Fear not, for God has placed a protection on your house until the Israelites come for you. Until then, the fallen ones cannot enter here. You shine with God's glory; they will flee from you."

Rahab turned around and placed her hand on the handle, slowly opening the door wider, she peered back outside.

All the creatures had disappeared.

She looked down the side streets a few more times before closing the door and facing Gabriel. "Where did they go?"

"They are still there. They are always there, but so are we. Sight does not bring belief, belief brings sight. God allowed you to see these things because you have believed on Him."

"Will I see Him?" Rahab asked.

"One day, yes, you will see Him face to face.

But that day is not today. There is still much more to your part of His plan."

Rahab bowed her head, closed her eyes, and smiled to herself.

When she opened her eyes and lifted her head, Gabriel was gone. She looked around for a few moments hoping the beautiful being would show himself again, but he did not.

Leaning up against the large wooden door, Rahab's family flashed in her mind.

"I don't know what I'm going to say to them," she said, hoping the messenger could still hear her and send some kind of answer. "They are never going to believe me."

A calming peace welled up inside her while her mind grew still.

"Got it," she said, as a smile crept across her face. "This is my chance and I'd better take it."

Rahab pulled her veil tight and grabbed her darkest cloak. Time was against her. She quickly ran through the streets of Jericho remembering where Alma had told her their older siblings had made their dwellings. Her breath caught at her next thought.

My parent's house.

If anyone was going to be the unmovable rock in this attempt, it would be her father. Rahab took in a deep breath but let it out quickly.

"If I'm going to do this right, I need to convince him first. The others will fall in line if they hear Father will come." She rubbed her forehead at the idea of facing the man she had not seen in years.

Chapter 13

*"When my father and my mother forsake me,
then the LORD will take me up."*
-PSALM 27:10

Pulling her veil even tighter around her face, Rahab quickly glanced over her shoulder to make sure no one had recognized her. Her golden eyes would have given her away in a moment. She knocked on the large wooden door quietly. She heard no movement. Taking a deep breath, Rahab knocked again louder to try to drown out the sound of her pounding heart.

The door flung open and a large man stood staring down at her.

"Father," she whispered and pushed herself in.

"Rahab?" The man spun around on his heels. "Is that you? What are you doing here? You know you are not welcome in this house."

Loosening her veil just enough to breathe easier, she inhaled. "I know, Father. But you are in danger and you need to come with me."

A loud laugh echoed off the stone dwelling. "Get out of here, you filthy woman." He pushed past her and headed for the next room.

"Father, please. I need to get you all to my home..." Rahab pleaded as she reached out for his arm.

"Home?" The massive frame of her father spun around to face her.

She saw the flames of anger creeping up in his dark eyes.

"You call that place of debauchery a home?" He grabbed her arm and began to pull her toward the door. "Well, you can just go right back to your *home*," he spat the word.

"Please, just listen to me for one moment. You are all in terrible danger!" She fought hard against him, but not enough to overcome his pull.

"What is going on in here?" a female voice yelled, as a hunched figure entered the room. "Get your hands off of her."

"Stay out of this. She does not belong here." Tzuri waved off his wife.

"Please, Mother. You're all in extreme danger." Rahab called over her father's arm. "Come with me and I will protect you."

"What are you talking about, child. What danger?" Liat crossed the room and stood beside her daughter.

"The city will be invaded soon and everyone will be destroyed," Rahab explained quickly, hoping to win over at least her mother.

"Ha, invaded? No one can invade Jericho." Her father chuckled as he tightened his grip on

Rahab's bicep.

"I have heard it with my own ears." She fought the tears of sorrow and pain. "There will be an invasion and lives will be taken." Rahab reached for her mother's hand and begged, "Please come with me. You will be safe in my home."

Tzuri raised Rahab's arm and began to lift her off the ground as he glared down into her shielded eyes. "What makes you think your house will be any safer than here in our own home?"

Rahab took a deep breath to steady herself. "I've made arrangements."

"I'm sure you have," Tzuri laughed, dropping her just low enough to show her he was still in control.

Rahab turned her face back to her mother. "Mother. I have had spies come to me and tell me what will be of Jericho."

Her mother took a deep breath. "Release her."

"You believe her?" Tzuri said with a shake of his head.

Liat looked deep into Rahab's eyes before answering, "Yes."

"If you believe her, then you can go with her. I'm not." Tzuri dropped Rahab.

She stumbled to catch herself.

Liat reached out to help steady her. "Rahab, what is it you need of us?"

As she wiped the dust off the hem of her dress, she answered, "We must gather all the family members together in my home. This must be done. Quickly, wake everyone in the house. I will go gather my sisters and brothers. Everyone who remains in my house will be spared." She turned back to face her father. "Anyone who is left outside of my home will not. I don't know when the invasion will come, but it is coming."

Tzuri turned his back on the two women.

"It will be done as you have spoken," Liat said and patted Rahab's arm.

Rahab looked at the back of her father and gently reached for his shoulder. "Father, please come with us. I do not wish to see you destroyed with the others of the city."

Her father's large frame turned toward her. "Why do you choose to show mercy upon us who have shown no mercy to you?"

"I show mercy because I have been shown mercy. The God of Israel has chosen to spare my life and, in return, my only request was to spare the life of my family. Father, if you ever wish to see all the years of your life, come to my house tonight." Not waiting for a reply, Rahab fixed her veil about her face so she could once again walk among the streets of Jericho." She turned back. "Alma?"

Liat waved her off. "She's sleeping, but I'll get her."

"Thank you."

It didn't take long before Rahab found herself standing at the door of her brother Even's house. He was older by a few years and reminded Rahab way too much of her father. Though he did not equal him in size, Even had the same stony stare of superiority which always made Rahab feel bad about herself, whether he meant to or not.

Rapping loudly, she knew he would be inside sitting aloft a pile of pillows while his quiet wife waited on him. She could picture them in her mind according to the stories Alma had told her. The woman would be flying swiftly about him like a shy dove to attend to his every whim. Rahab did not envy such a position; nor did she require one.

It was the small body who opened the door.

Rahab stood staring at the downturned face of her sister-in-law.

Unsure of what to do next in the shock of seeing a well-known harlot standing at her door, the frightened creature hesitated.

Rahab could only guess at the conflicting thoughts the woman was probably thinking. It was customary to invite any calling visitor in for food and lodging, but one with Rahab's reputation would undoubtedly raise neighboring eyebrows. Family was to be welcomed with open arms, but this family had made it quite clear that Rahab would never be counted among them.

Feeling the growing tension in the woman whose husband's anger toward his wife's hesitation would be mounting; Rahab took matters into her own hands and pushed past the statue.

"Brother?" she called, knowing he would

remain seated, but wishing to warn him of her presence.

"Rahab?" she heard his deep voice call.

Finding him just as she had imagined, Even sat with bottom jaw ajar and a bowl in his hand. "What is the meaning of this intrusion?"

"You are in danger, Brother," she said as she bowed and knelt before him.

"I have done nothing to bring danger upon myself," he said with reassurance.

"We are all in danger."

Even huffed and then stuffed a handful of flatbread into his waiting mouth.

Rahab reached for the bowl in her brother's hand. "Jericho's pride has cast an impending lot of destruction and I do not wish to tiptoe through the blood of my family as it runs in the streets."

He eyed her while he chewed. "How have you come by this information?"

"Spies."

Even rolled his eyes and pulled for his bowl.

"Honest, Brother. The information is valid." She reached over to stop his arm. "Jericho will fall."

"And what is your brilliant plan for saving Jericho?"

Rahab thought. She never intended on saving Jericho. It was just a city. Made of stone walls and mud. No. It wasn't Jericho she was looking to protect; it was the people whose blood ran through her; her family. Staring into the dark brown eyes of her brother, she sighed deeply. "Jericho will fall, but we don't have to fall with it. Come with me, you..." Rahab paused. She knew the quiet woman, though out of sight, was close enough to hear every word. "...and your family. If you stay in my house, you will all be protected when the Wanderers invade."

"Wanderers? You mean those foolish people from the desert?"

Rahab nodded.

"That is what this is all about?" He squinted his eyes as he pulled his arm away from her.

"They have already destroyed great cities and Jericho is next."

"Yes, I've heard about them." Even's eyes darted away.

"Then you know the stories of the strength of their god."

Even rubbed on his dark, curly beard. "When do we have to decide?"

"Right now."

"The invasion is tonight then?" He looked around for his sword, which had never been used.

"I'm not sure of when the attack will come," she said, shaking her head.

"Then why charge into my home and cause such a stir?" he questioned.

Rahab's head popped up to look her brother in the face. "Not knowing is the urgency. What if the night is tonight?"

Even tapped his index finger against the clay

bowl a few times, but never broke his sister's stare. "Tira," he called and waited to hear her footsteps approach. "Wake the children. Get them dressed and pack a few sets of clothes. Gather your things and then pack up some of our food. We are leaving tonight." Even ordered, with his gaze still locked on Rahab. "If you are wrong, dear sister..."

"I'm not."

Chapter 14

"For thou hast been a shelter for me, and a strong tower from the enemy."
-PSALM 61:3

Later that night, Rahab heard the first knocking on the Inn door.

"Should we be expecting visitors?" Tzuri's words dripped with disgust as he entered.

Rahab did not respond to her father's prodding as she welcomed in the slow trickle of people.

After gathering her bother Even and his family, Rahab had made her way to the homes of her two sisters. She convinced them to seek shelter in her house.

Each family group had made themselves comfortable at tables in the empty dining room.

"Where are all your workers?" Alma asked.

"I sent them home. I also cleared all the rooms so there will be plenty of rooms for everyone. It wasn't easy, but the Inn is all clear."

"What about the..."

"The women?"

Alma nodded.

"I made arrangements with another Inn on the other side of town." Rahab shared a smile with her sister before closing the door behind her. She placed a large beam across the door.

"Are you locking us in?" Tzuri asked.

"More like keeping everyone else out."

Liat tilted her head.

"The spies instructed that I gather my family here in my home. All who would be found behind this door...," she patted it, "...would be spared when they return. All those outside would not. I don't want to take the chance of one of you being outside this door when they come for us. It will remain locked until then."

Rahab helped Alma show their mother to a seat. She searched around the room and counted heads.

Ten adults and seven children. Rahab paused. *Wait. No. That count is wrong.*

Rahab looked over at Alma who was holding Shira's daughter. Alma would still be counted as a child by her family. She was old enough to be an adult, but remained unmarried.

I wonder if any of them count me as a child. Nine adults and eight children.

She gazed around at the high stone walls. Not knowing how long they would all have to remain together, Rahab hoped the walls could take the tension and pressure that bubbled just below the surface of her family. There were many unspoken issues and concerns waiting in the dark like a wild animal ready to pounce on its next meal.

Peering around one more time, Rahab giggled to herself. She toyed with the idea of her family's tension being the ram which would bring down the walls of Jericho.

"Who else is hungry?" she said, moving toward the kitchen.

Calls and murmurs filled the air.

"Alma, could you give me a hand?" Rahab said. "I've got lots of food cooking in the kitchen. We seem to have some hungry people here."

The petite young girl raced to the next room, ready to serve.

"What can I do?" Liat called from her seat at one of the tables.

"Nothing, Mother." Rahab stepped back into the dining room. "You just stay comfortable and I'll have Alma bring you a bowl."

"If you're sure," the old woman said, easing herself back.

Rahab looked upon the aging body of her mother with fresh eyes. Liat had her dark blue veil loosely hanging about her neck in the presence of her family. It allowed Rahab to see the grayish-white which had overtaken the black curly hair she remembered. Skin that once seemed softer than lamb's skin now looked leathery and worn by the elements and darkened by the sun. Her mother's eyes had always been filled with such life. Now they were dimmed and lacked their former strength. Rahab quickly realized how much Liat quietly depended on other people in the room to hand her things or tell her what was around her.

Just then, Alma flew into the room.

Before Rahab could say anything to her, Alma rushed to Liat. She placed the older woman's hands on either side of a clay bowl.

"Careful, it is still warm, Mother. Eat it slowly." Alma said before she ran back to the kitchen.

On the next few trips, Alma made sure all the adults had enough food and the little ones had everything they needed before sitting herself down to eat her own bowl of food.

Rahab walked over to her sister and sat. She nudged her with her elbow and asked, "How long has mother been like that?"

Alma followed Rahab's gaze to the place where Liat sat and then back again. "Been like what?"

Rahab shrugged and smiled. "Old?"

Alma stifled a laugh and then elbowed her older sister. "She's not old."

"You know what I mean. She seems...I don't know. So needy."

The younger woman looked over at their mother. "It's getting worse, but it has always been this way."

Rahab thought often about the family she had left. It was foolish for her to believe they would have all remained the same. Glancing around, she realized just how much each of them had changed.

Her oldest brother, Even, had grown into a man before her eyes. She remembered his face looking down on her when they were children. He reminded her so much of their father.

Rahab was the next oldest and, with the exception of Alma, she was not sure how any of them viewed her.

Her thoughts went briefly to the face of the missing child. Rahab wished desperately that Noda was sitting among them at that moment.

Would he have been tall? Would his gentle disposition have been pounded out by a rough life? She shook the painful thoughts out of her head.

Next in line was Shira. She took after their mother more than the other girls. Her stocky build was strange for a female, but she kept to herself and busied herself with her family. Rahab always saw her as the child her parents had to replace Noda.

Hed was the fourth child and middle sister. Rahab saw her as the child her parents had to replace her. Needless to say, they did not get along very well. Hed was not as beautiful as everyone claimed Rahab to be, but she was pretty in her own right, even with some of their father's harder features. Her dark olive skin was beautiful to look upon without making an innocent man blush. Like all the children, she shared the dark brown eyes with their father and mother. Except for the honey-colored eyes Rahab had all to herself.

Alma, who was born long after Rahab left,

seemed to be the binding which held them together. She was sweet and saw only the best in people. Even if the worst was staring her in the face. Her mild olive skin shone as if it were polished and her brown eyes of toasted cinnamon made Rahab wonder if Alma had not been a physically born child of her parents. Instead, it was as if someone had uniquely formed her and placed her in a family that would never be good enough for her. She laughed often enough to have lines at the corners of her eyes, even for one so young. When she walked, which was less often than running, Alma was always up on her toes, as if she was ready to sprint into action at any moment like a wildcat.

Rahab looked down at her hands to see worn leather just starting to show where soft flesh once stood. She had not been the hardest working woman in the city. Her hands were beginning to wear faster than ever before, with all the sewing and dyeing Rahab had done to keep up with demand. Smiling to herself, a feeling of pride and accomplishment filled her heart.

Alma's right. It is nice to do honorable work.

Chapter 15

"And they went, and came unto the mountain, and abode there three days, until the pursuers were returned: and the pursuers sought them throughout all the way, but found them not."
-JOSHUA 2:22

Salmon turned to Caleb and asked, "Do you think it is safe?" before his gaze returned to the mouth of the cave.

Caleb stood up and headed toward the opening. He looked out over the desert. "Looks safe."

"It's been three days."

"Right. They would've given up looking for us and gone back to Jericho by now," Caleb said as he grabbed his cloak.

The two men set out down the mountain and back to their camp.

When they reached the vast tent city, the onlookers cheered as the spies headed toward Joshua's tent.

"Welcome," Joshua said, as he embraced the two men. "Sit. Tell me what you witnessed in

Jericho."

Caleb sat down on a stack of pillows before he began, "Joshua, the city of Jericho is a strong and well-guarded one. The walls are so thick; three camels could walk across it side by side. The army is strong and numerous."

Joshua listened intently and rubbed his dark beard that was just beginning to show some gray.

"Yes, the walls are thick and the soldiers are many, but our God is stronger than any wall built by the hands of man," Salmon interrupted. "And did He not conquer the Egyptians on our behalf?"

Caleb turned to his companion. "Faith flows from your mouth."

"Our God is great. He has shown us that over and over again. I trust Him and believe when He says we will conquer Jericho."

"True. How hard can it be to conquer a city whose king's men listen to a prostitute?" Caleb smiled and elbowed Salmon's leg.

Blood rushed to Salmon's cheeks as the remembrance of Rahab's face flooded his mind. Luckily for him, Joshua was looking at the floor and stroking his beard in thought. He was not so fortunate to escape the glances of Caleb, who was stifling a chuckle.

"Prostitute?" Joshua finally asked.

"Yes, Sir. We found shelter with a prostitute in Jericho," Caleb answered. "She told us that her city has heard all our God has done for us. She was in reverence over His strength and testified to our

God being the true God. The harlot told us that the people's hearts melted at the stories of our God and the men have become afraid because of what they have heard."

"Do you trust her?" Joshua lifted his eyebrow.

"With my life," Salmon answered without waiting for Caleb.

Joshua rose from his pillows and paced around the tent. "Truly, the Lord has delivered Jericho into our hands because even the people fear us."

"Give the signal and we will be ready to march," Caleb said. His hand flew to his sword and he rose to his feet in the same movement.

"We will leave at sunrise. Spread the word," Joshua commanded.

"To Jericho," Caleb shouted as he lifted his sword over his head.

Joshua turned to him. "No. To Jordan first."

Salmon lifted his head toward Joshua.

"Sir?" Caleb lowered his sword slowly. "I do not understand. God has given us Jericho for the taking..."

"And we will. The Lord's way. He has laid the plan out before me and we shall follow it."

"I understand," Caleb said as he returned his sword to his sheath.

"Excuse me while I finalize the march," Joshua said, as he walked back to his table of scrolls and maps.

Salmon stood, bowed to Joshua, and headed out of the tent.

"You are thinking about her, aren't you?" Caleb stood shoulder to shoulder with Salmon and looked at the horizon. "The prostitute?"

Salmon allowed his eyes to fall to his sandaled feet and kicked the dirt a few times before answering, "Yes."

The two men stood in silence for a few moments.

"There is something about her. I can't put my finger on it."

"She's a harlot," Caleb joked.

Salmon nodded and looked back out to the vast desert. "Yes, but she is more than that."

After three days of camping at Jordan, the leaders of the army marched through the people giving orders handed down from Joshua. "When you see the ark of the covenant of the Lord your God, follow it," they shouted to the people.

Joshua followed behind the officers shouting, "Cleanse yourselves this day for tomorrow the Lord will do wonders among you."

The following morning, the priests took up the ark and headed toward the Jordan River. While they went down toward the water, the people came from their tents and watched. As soon as the feet of the priests came near the water's edge, the water began to pull back.

The people walked curiously toward the river. Everyone watched as the water rose straight in the air as it pulled away from the ground and made a wide path in front of the Ark of the Covenant straight to the other side of the river.

"Look," someone called from the crowd.

Wherever the water had stepped aside, the ground was solid and dry.

The priests walked out into the parted river and marched toward the other side, but stopped halfway through the river.

"It is just like our parents told us about when they left Egypt," an older man cried from the crowd. "The water is standing on its side to give us a path."

Remembering Joshua's instructions from the previous day, the people gathered their supplies and followed the priests through the water and crossed over to the other side.

It took hours for all the people of Israel to cross over the river.

Once everyone had crossed the Jordan, Joshua called out, "You chosen twelve, pick a boulder from the bottom of the Jordan for each of you and place it over there near where we are going to camp this night."

Twelve men, one from each of the tribes, did just as Joshua commanded.

When they had completed their task, Joshua again spoke to the crowd, "We do this so that all of our children will know what God has done for us this day."

The people of Israel cheered.

Joshua turned to the priests who stood in the midst of the Jordan, standing on dry ground.

"Come up out of the Jordan," he called.

Once the last foot of the priests left the bottom of the Jordan, the water returned to its place while the people settled for the night.

In the morning, Joshua gathered the people together to make an announcement. "God has given a final instruction before we are to head toward Jericho."

"You want to do what?" Salmon asked Joshua, who stood in his tent with a flint knife in his right hand.

"It's God instructions. All those born in the wilderness must be circumcised before we enter into the land the Lord has given us."

"That is supposed to be done to infants."

"I understand your concern. No one has performed the practice while we have marched in the wilderness. It's part of our disobedience. We've got to set things right with God."

Salmon shook his head. "I don't know about this."

"Trust me. I know what I'm doing."

The next day, Salmon heard Caleb's voice outside his tent. "Enter."

"I came to check on you." Caleb sat beside Salmon's mat.

A shiver rose up Salmon's back. "Not so bad."

Caleb reached over and grabbed a damp cloth. He wiped Salmon's brow. "You look like one of the people with the serpent sickness."

"That well?"

Caleb chuckled. "At least you have your sense of humor.

Salmon smiled, but another tremor shook through him. He saw the fear in his friend's eyes. "How long?"

"Usually a week for the fever to pass. Maybe another for the swelling to go away. It can be rough. Especially the older you are." Caleb dipped the cloth into some water and then wiped Salmon's brow again. "Why do you think God told us to do this when a male is only eight days old. It's much easier on their little bodies."

Salmon closed his eyes.

"It will pass."

He looked at Caleb.

"It will pass. You will be up marching next to me soon enough."

Salmon nodded.

"Joshua is giving everyone time. We are not moving until every male is well enough to travel."

"That's good news."

"Rest, my friend. I will come back to check on you before nightfall."

Chapter 16

"But his flesh upon him shall have pain, and his soul within him shall mourn."
-JOB 14:22

"This is crazy," Tzuri spoke up in Rahab's Inn. "We have been sitting here for two weeks and nothing has happened." He walked across the room and leaned against the stone wall.

Rahab glared over at her father from her place near the window.

"I'm serious, Daughter. If something doesn't happen soon, I'm going home," he said as he stomped his foot.

"I'm with Father," Even said. "I think all this talk has gotten to everyone's heads. The whole city is locked up tight and no one is allowed to go out or come in the gates of Jericho."

Liat brushed Alma's hair and sighed.

"You too, Mother?" Rahab asked while staring out the window.

"Well, if anyone were to ask me," Shira began.

"No one did ask you," Alma answered.

Shira huffed. "Watch your tongue, young

one."

"Enough, girls. We are all exhausted, but we are safe," Liat said.

Hed walked in from the other room and placed her hand on her father's shoulder. "Everything will be alright, Father."

"No, Daughter, it will not be alright. We have been crammed in this house for weeks now. There is no sign of Rahab's army anywhere."

"I know they are out there," Rahab whispered, but didn't care if anyone heard her.

"When? Did your spies not share this information with you?" Tzuri asked.

Rahab spun around toward her father. "You know, dear Father, I grow tired of your childish temper and judgment. If it weren't for me sticking my neck out for you..."

"Rahab," Liat screamed.

She bit her lip and shot a glance at her mother, who could not see her from across the room. "I do grow tired of him, Mother."

"Hold your tongue, Daughter," she ordered.

"I will not."

Alma gasped.

Even moved between Tzuri and Rahab. "You will hold your tongue, Woman."

Rahab felt the heat of anger rising inside her and used it to open her mouth. "I will speak. This is my home."

Even raised his hand to strike her, but Tzuri grabbed it.

The younger man stood shocked. He desperately searched his father's face for an explanation.

"Peace."

Even squinted his eyes. He ripped his wrist out of Tzuri's grasp and stormed out of the room.

Tzuri looked over at Rahab. "Speak."

Pausing to consider the beating she would endure for her words, Rahab decided it better to speak and be punished than to hold her words and regret letting the opportunity pass without a chance of it coming again. "Things have happened in this family. I think we need to discuss them," she said.

Tzuri nodded slightly.

Rahab took a breath to steady her anger into focus. "I don't agree with some choices which were made concerning Noda."

The sound of the unspoken name made each member of the family gasp in unison.

"Rahab, don't," Liat's voice cracked with the plea.

"I have to, Mother. It's not fair that he had to die in my place."

"What?" Alma questioned.

Liat cooed her youngest child as she covered Alma's ears.

Alma pulled away from her mother and slowly rose.

Walking over to Rahab with unsteady steps, she stared at her older sister. "What did you say?"

"It wasn't fair for Noda to die for me," Rahab repeated slowly.

"Noda didn't die for you. His death was an accident."

Rahab shook her head. Looking over to where her father stood, she saw he had turned his shoulder to them. She watched her mother grasp the air around her, trying to catch Alma. "What did you tell her?" Rahab questioned.

Tzuri closed his eyes and held his mouth shut.

Alma looked at each person in the room as the majority hung their heads in shame. She glanced back at Rahab whose eyes were boring a hole in their father's back. "What happened to Noda?"

"What story did they tell you?" Rahab did not break her stare.

Alma thought for a moment. "Noda had an accident. He was trampled by a wild horse because he left Mother's side in the market."

Rahab shook her head. "No. He didn't."

Liat began to sob.

"What happened to him?" Alma questioned.

Looking into the innocent eyes of her younger sister, Rahab sighed. "They told you that to keep you safe. So you would stay with Mother in the marketplace. Noda was not killed by a horse." Rahab could feel the anger rising up inside her again. "He was murdered at the hands of your parents."

Liat whaled.

Alma quickly looked to both her parents and

back at Rahab. "What?" The word shook out of Alma's mouth.

Clearing her throat and trying fiercely to stuff down her own rage, Rahab went on, "When I was born, the two of them decided to choose me as a sacrifice for the harvest. Before that happened, I..." She paused, searching Alma's sweet eyes.

Can she handle her world being torn down at the hands of her own sister?

"I was raped."

Alma tilted her head in confusion.

"Two men defiled me when I had gotten lost in the city one night. I had been playing with friends instead of home doing my chores," Rahab said, hoping to bring some ounce of peace to her mother's heart. "Once the elders found out, I was no longer acceptable. Father and Mother had to look to their next child. Noda." She smiled picturing her brother's face. "He was still small enough and pure enough. He would be welcomed. So, *they...*" she spat the word, "...turned him over to the elders. I watched his tiny body burn in the altar fire."

Alma let out the breath she had been holding. "So, that's the truth?"

"Yes," Rahab said. "That's the truth. I became a temple priestess because the elders said I was not pure enough to be burned to feed the hunger of the gods. Nor was I clean enough to be given over for the appetite of a husband. Alma knows how I got here, but the rest of you don't. I came to this

Inn after being kidnapped by a customer and escaping. I couldn't go back to that Temple."

Taking a deep breath, Alma reached up and hugged her sister's neck. "I'm sorry for what happened to you," she whispered in her ear.

Rahab's eyes burned to be released of their tears, but they did not come.

Pulling back, she said, "Thank you for telling me the truth."

Rahab nodded.

Moving across the room, Alma gently hugged her sobbing mother and patted her head. Then she went to where her father still stood bracing himself against the stone wall. Reaching up, she placed her palm on his cheek. "It's alright, father."

The large man slid to the ground in a heap.

Alma looked down at him and patted his head. "I know you were just trying to protect me. There is nothing that can be done about the past." With that, she left the room.

After a long pause of emotion, Rahab glanced between her parents. "How could you tell her such a lie?" she asked, not waiting for them to respond before she followed after Alma.

"Alma?" Rahab called.

"Here I am."

Rahab sat beside her sister.

"I am sorry for what happened to you."

Rahab nodded. "Me too."

"Why didn't you ever tell me yourself?"

"I'm not sure." She shrugged. "You're young.

I didn't want you to know about that kind of thing. I didn't want to scare you."

"I'm not as young as you think, Sister."

Rahab patted her knee.

"I'm not. I should have been married by now."

"I know."

"They treat me like an infant. Mother keeps talking Father out of making plans for me. I've heard them speak in hushed tones when they think I'm sleeping."

"She loves you. She's doesn't want you to go away."

"I'm not a child, Rahab."

"I know."

"Mother calls for him in her sleep."

Rahab flinched.

"It must have been awful for her to give him up."

"It was. I wish it had not been necessary."

"I don't."

Rahab looked at her.

"If you had been burned instead, then you wouldn't be here with me. I'd be stuck with Hed and Shira as big sisters to look up to."

"At least they are honorable sisters for you to look up to."

"But would they be strong enough to save us?" Alma met her eyes. "Strong enough to believe in a God we can't see?"

Chapter 17

"And the captain of the LORD'S host said unto Joshua, 'Loose thy shoe from off thy foot; for the place whereon thou standest is holy.' And Joshua did so."
-JOSHUA 5:15

Salmon found his way over to his best friend, Caleb. "What is going on today?"

"Joshua wants us to observe the Passover before we head out. Come. Sit with me, my friend."

Salmon nodded. "Thank you."

Caleb stoked the fire that cooked his lamb as Salmon sat down. "Here," he handed Salmon some unleavened bread.

Salmon smiled as he ate the bread and shared in the simple meal.

The next morning, Salmon woke and walked out of his tent.

Many people were already out and searching the ground.

"It's gone," Salmon whispered to himself. He looked around and instantly noticed what was missing.

Caleb came running up to his friend. "It's all gone, Salmon."

"I see."

"Where do you think the manna went? It has been here exactly as God promised since we left Egypt. Where is it now?"

"I don't know." Salmon watched the faces of the people turn from curious to fright. "We need to go to Joshua."

They found their leader pacing in his tent.

"Joshua, do you know what is going on outside," Caleb said as soon as they entered.

"God has ceased the manna," Joshua said.

"God has done this thing?" Caleb asked.

Joshua looked up at his warriors with widened eyes.

"Should we be worried?" Salmon asked.

"God spoke to me this very morning saying that He would stop sending manna from Heaven. All of our future meals will come from the land of Canaan."

Salmon and Caleb exchanged a glance before returning their focus toward their leader.

"We will soon be marching forward." Joshua placed a hand on Caleb's shoulder. "Prepare for war, men."

Another week had passed for the people gathered in Rahab's house. Though many still held to the unspoken way of how the family ran, everyone could feel the shift of power. Noda's death was no longer a hidden shame. Rahab had admitted out loud what had happened to her and the course her life had taken because of it.

The family was scattered around the large living room on the second floor of the Inn. Each busied themselves with something. The men busied their hands with some kind of wood or metal object, fashioning it into this or that. The women were either preparing food or hemming a garment.

Rahab sat perched on the ledge of her large window which looked out into the desert. She held a new dress which was quickly taking shape in her hands.

Tzuri strutted about the room like a rooster counting his hens. "How long has it been since we locked ourselves in here?"

"It is nearing a month, Father," Shira answered.

He huffed a few times as he continued to pace. "Surprises me we have been able to hold back any night visitors this long."

Rahab looked at her father out of the corner of her eye.

Fingering a curtain which hung on one side of the room, Tzuri continued, "All of these things, bought with dirty money."

Rahab's siblings watched their father, but none dared to speak in Rahab's defense. They knew what she did and none agreed with it.

All of them except Alma, who found the strength to speak. "Not all of it."

"Pardon me?" Tzuri spun around to face his youngest daughter.

Alma gulped down the lump in her throat. "Not everything in Rahab's house was bought with harlot wages."

Tzuri waved his hand around in a circle. "My girl, your sister is a harlot. If we are going to get all the truth out in the open, let us get that fact straight in your young mind."

"You're wrong, Father."

Gasps and mutters filled the air.

Tzuri's mouth hung open. "You know nothing, young one."

Alma cleared her throat. "I may not know as much as you, Father, but I know more about Rahab than you will ever care to learn."

"Well then," he chuckled. "By all means. Please, enlighten me."

She crossed the room from her spot in the corner to stand beside Rahab in the window. "Sister gave up being a harlot months ago. I have been helping her sell her garments in the market to make money so she did not have to sell her body anymore." Picking up the garment out of Rahab's lap, Alma showed the dress around the room. "She is terrific."

Tzuri left the room with a snort.

Rahab slid off the ledge and followed her sister across the room.

Alma showed Hed the dress Rahab had been putting together.

"It is good, sister," Hed agreed as she pulled on the seams of the garment.

Rahab smiled.

"She can make anything," Alma continued on as she pointed out many of the items which filled Rahab's home.

"What made you give up being a harlot? I'm sure it paid better than selling dresses," Hed asked.

Rahab looked to the floor.

"Tell her, Sister," Alma urged. "Tell her what you told me."

"Tell me what?" Hed shook her head.

"One night, I couldn't sleep. I went up to the roof to think. I was dreaming about all the stories of the Wanderers and their god."

"I've heard them," Hed said.

"It was so strange. When I think about their god...I don't know." She shrugged. "I just have so much peace. I do believe their god is the one true God. I didn't want to be a harlot anymore. I wanted to be free from that life."

"I'm glad you found peace, Sister." Hed placed her hand on Rahab's shoulder. She stepped away to check on her children.

Alma moved closer to Rahab. "Why didn't you tell her the rest?"

"About what?"

"The light being and the unseen army in the desert?"

"No one would believe me. They never believed me about the other creatures."

"I believe you," Alma insisted.

"It wouldn't matter. They believe in their own gods. But maybe, when we are all safe on the other side of this, they will see the God of the Wanderers and His power."

"I know I can't wait to see that." Alma clapped.

Joshua went out before the people and headed toward Jericho. Alone. He made it halfway between his camp and Jericho's gates before he stopped dead in his tracks.

A bright light temporarily blinded him.

Removing his hands from his eyes, he saw a tall being standing a stone's throw away from him with a sword in his right hand.

Joshua made his way toward the man and asked, "Are you for us or against us?"

"Neither, but as the captain of the host of the Lord am I come," the large creature answered.

Joshua crumbled to the ground and trembled. When he could lift his face out of the sand, he asked, "What do you have to say unto your servant?"

"Loose your sandals from your feet, for you are standing on holy ground," the captain said.

Carefully bringing his feet up to his hands, Joshua removed his sandals and stood, but the captain had gone.

"See, Jericho is shut up tight because they have heard all I have done for My children. I have given Jericho over into your hands," a familiar voice spoke to Joshua.

Although he saw no one, he knew it was the Lord.

"You shall compass the city, all the men of war and the priests with the ark, and this you shall do for six days without making a sound. The seven priests shall carry seven ram's horns. On the seventh day, they shall march seven times around the city and then tell the priests to blow their horns. When you hear the blast of the horns, all the people shall shout with a great shout and the wall of the city shall fall down. The soldiers shall ascend up the walls and take the city.

"Kill every living thing in the city and take only what I tell you. Take all the silver, gold, and vessels of brass and iron and put them in the treasury of the Lord. Take Rahab, all her family, and everything of hers. Place them outside your camp, but within your protection."

Joshua ran back to the camp and told his officers all the Lord had told him.

They gathered together the men of war, the priests, and the people and began the march toward Jericho.

As they came over the last sand dune, Salmon smiled. He spotted the window with the crimson cord blowing in the wind. He could barely see her face, but Salmon knew Rahab was there watching him. His heart pounded loudly in his chest. He couldn't be sure if it was the excitement of the march or the face of the woman who had sent the blood rushing to his face the moment he first saw her that pushed him forward, but Salmon marched faster toward the high walls.

After Salmon helped drive in the last stake of Joshua's tent in the sand, he made his way to the edge of the large tent city. He stared at the massive walls of Jericho for a long time before returning to his own tent.

The plan Joshua had laid out before they left seemed crazy at the time, it felt even wilder now that they were actually going through with it. He looked up at the tan-colored skin that made up the ceiling of his small tent. "I don't know what you're doing, God, but I'm ready when you are to take down Jericho," he prayed, before rolling over and falling asleep.

Chapter 18

"And the city shall be accursed, even it, and all that are therein, to the LORD: only Rahab the harlot shall live, she and all that are with her in the house, because she hid the messengers that we sent."
-JOSHUA 6:17

"I don't understand why we have to be locked up here either," Even spoke in a low voice to his wife.

Rahab had listened to lots of grumblings from her family over the past month. With the rise of each question, she felt her own frustration grow.

"How much longer do you think it will be?" Alma asked concerned.

"I don't know," she hissed.

Alma's head popped up from her sewing.

"Sorry." Rahab instantly regretted speaking to her closest ally in the world with such hatred.

She nodded a few times before looking back to her work.

"Rahab, don't you think we should go to the altar today?" Shira walked up to Rahab and stood over her. "It has been weeks since any of us offered up a sacrifice. The gods' anger will be growing hot."

"We're not going anywhere," she answered, trying to steady her voice.

Shira tilted her head at her sister. "Who knows what will happen to us if the gods act on their anger."

Rahab took a deep breath and said, "I don't care what your false gods do with their anger."

Hed gasped from across the room. "What are you talking about? We all serve the same gods. Though, I'm sure they have turned a deaf ear to you a long time ago."

Rahab rose to her feet and clasped her shaking hands. "I believe in the God of the Wanderers."

Laughter exploded from Shira's mouth. "Is that the reason for all of this?" She waved her hand toward the open window. "Those desert fools?"

"I believe the God they follow is the one true God," Rahab said with downcast eyes.

"'The one true God?' What does that even mean?" Tzuri questioned nearby.

Rahab turned her head to look at her father. "It means that all the other gods in this world are false. The God who leads the Wanderers is the true, one and only. He is God in Heaven above and of the earth below."

"What has their god done for you?" Even broke into the discussion.

Rahab looked out the large open window. "He does not have to do anything for me to be powerful."

"And what of our gods and goddesses? Do they not have power? What of Astarte? The goddess our family has served for generations." Shira asked.

"Power? What power?" Rahab rushed toward her. "If they had power, then why didn't they stop Noda from being burned. If Astarte watches over her daughter, then where was she when I laid helpless in the street after being ravaged by brutal beasts."

"Where was the god of the Wanderers," Shira snapped back.

Rahab clenched her jaw.

"The gods anger against you was made known," she continued.

"I do not care whether or not Astarte lives. She has no power in my life." She curled her fingers into fists. "I choose to believe the powerful God who leads the Wanderers through the desert and toward Jericho is the ultimate authority in the world and elsewhere."

"What if your precious spies never come back for you?" Shira teased.

Rahab thought on the idea. "Then so be it. But I will stand ready, waiting to hear them marching to rescue us from impending destruction."

Shira laughed. "Sure. I can hear them now. A large army marching through the sand coming for the harlot Rahab." She held her hand in front of her as if holding a shield. "Let us go and bring down the walls of Jericho to snatch up the dirty woman of the night."

"Stop it, Shira," Alma lashed.

Shira held out her other hand as if holding onto a heavy sword, lifting it high in the air, she spoke in a deep voice. "Let us risk life and limb to take a filthy, fallen woman out of a city of honorable girls."

"I'm warning you, Shira," Rahab warned her. "If you don't stop right now..."

"Shh...Do you hear that?" Hed said as she headed to look out the window.

"That's enough, Hed." Rahab whipped around to face her. "Stop joking. I am so tired of none of you believing me. If any of you want to leave, then just leave and stop mocking me." She headed toward the door and reached for the beam across the door.

"Wait." Alma touched Rahab's shoulder. "I hear it too."

Rahab turned her face to the ceiling and closed her eyes. Directing all of her focus to the sounds outside, she heard the faint shuffling of thousands of feet marching in the sand. Rahab rushed up the steps to look out the window. She searched the open desert.

Over the horizon came a crowd of strange faces marching toward Jericho.

She examined each face until her eyes landed on a familiar one. Her heart began to gallop.

Salmon was out in front, helping lead the

group growing larger with each passing moment.

"I would never have believed it unless I saw it with my own eyes," Tzuri said, as he stood next to Rahab and watched the army head toward his beloved city.

"I told you they would come." Rahab looked up into her father's eyes.

"They may be coming, but they won't make it past the walls," he sneered.

"I believe they will," Rahab said, glancing back to find the one face in the crowd she wanted to come for her.

"So, this is the army who will destroy Jericho?"

Rahab did not give him the satisfaction of a response. Instead, she kept her eyes on Salmon's face. "Here they come," Rahab said. Her heart pounded so loud, she feared everyone in the house would hear it.

As the men of war passed by, Rahab noticed there was another group of people following the army. They were men dressed in long, white robes carrying large horns in their hands which they blew as they marched.

Behind the group of robed men were several more men. They were dressed in the same robes, but were carrying a large box covered by a blue cloth. It sat on golden poles.

The box of death.

After them were women, children, and older men following behind.

"They are so quiet," Alma remarked.

Rahab looked over her shoulder at her sister.

Tzuri walked to the other side of the room and leaned against the wall. He let a long pause go before asking, "What are they doing?"

"Marching," Rahab said.

"Just marching?" Kalil, Shira's husband, asked.

Rahab nodded, "Just marching."

"Some army," Tzuri shrugged.

It didn't take long before the Wanderers had made a complete circle around Jericho.

Rahab watched in horror as the people, who she believed were coming to rescue her, seemed to be retreating.

Tzuri huffed beside her. "Some battle plan."

"I don't understand," she whispered to the sand.

The army of people stopped just before the horizon and began to spread out across the open desert like a blanket.

"What are they doing?" Rahab shook her head in confusion.

The following morning, Rahab was stirred by the sound of marching. She rushed to the large window and sat on the ledge to watch the Wanderers progressed under her.

When will they strike?

As the group completed their circle around the

city, they again headed away from Jericho and toward the tent city they had built out in the sand.

The tension was thick in Rahab's house. It only magnified in the following days as they watched the events unfold outside the window of the Inn.

After days of witnessing the Wanderers march around Jericho, Rahab's family grew restless.

"They are never going to do anything more than march," Even said what everyone else was thinking.

"I wonder if this is how they took down Bashan," Tzuri spoke up.

Rahab shot him a glance that would have threatened a lesser man.

It was enough to at least quiet him.

Watching as long as she could to see Salmon near the front of the army, Rahab followed the line of people march around Jericho. When they finished, the people headed back to camp for the sixth night in a row.

"When are they going to attack?" Kalil asked Rahab.

"Perhaps they are waiting for just the right moment," Rahab turned to face her brother-in-law.

"What exactly are they waiting on?"

Rahab turned back to watch the dust from the

last man settle back down. "God will show them."

"You really believe in their God?"

Rahab took a deep breath before answering, "My dear brother, before this is over, you will too."

Kalil shook his head and walked away.

Rahab checked on each family in the rooms of the Inn. After the last one, she sighed and turned back to the window. She closed her eyes and then opened them wide, but she didn't see the host that Gabriel had shown her before. Though she could not see them with her eyes, she knew in her heart that they were still there, standing guard. Soon they would be attacking Jericho with the children of Israel.

When, God? When?

The next morning, Rahab woke and headed straight to the window to catch a glimpse of Salmon before he passed by. She watched the group march under her window and waited for the moment when the army would come back to the place they began.

As she ate her morning meal, Rahab wondered when the day would finally come for Jericho to fall into the hands of the Israelites. When she had finished eating, she ran to her familiar spot on the window ledge to see Salmon's face one more time.

Peering out the window, she saw Salmon come into view, but he did not follow their leader back toward their camp as he had done the past six days. Instead, the army marched back under Rahab's window and around the city again.

"What are those people doing now?" Tzuri asked as he listened to the sounds of thousands of strangers marching around outside.

"They are marching," Rahab answered.

"I know that," he said, heading to the window. "I thought they had already passed by."

"They did. They are going around again."

"Again?" Alma asked as she stood beside Rahab and peered out the window.

Rahab pointed to the front of the army as they rounded the edge of the wall. "Again."

Chapter 19

"He cast upon them the fierceness of his anger,
wrath, and indignation, and trouble, by sending
evil angels among them."
-PSALM 78:49

For the rest of the day, Rahab sat on her window ledge and watched the army march around the city.

"How many does that make?" Alma asked.

"They are heading around for the seventh time," Rahab replied.

"Seven times? They've never done that many before."

"I know."

Alma stretched out the window. "The sun is getting low in the sky."

Rahab nodded.

She saw Salmon's face come around the corner. She fully excepted him to turn his back once again on Jericho and head to his camp in the desert. But he didn't. Instead, the group suddenly came to a complete stop.

Rahab stood.

"What's going on?" Alma asked, coming to sit next to her.

"I don't know. They just stopped."

"Look," Alma pointed.

The men in white robes brought the ram's horns to their lips and blew.

Rahab and Alma covered their ears.

Shouts came from every direction.

"What is all that noise?" Shira called from the next room.

"It's the people," Alma yelled over the deafening sound. "They are screaming."

Rahab's family came running into the room to see for themselves.

When the breath of the people below had given out, the silence made everyone in Rahab's house pause.

The silence lasted only a moment before it was broken by a loud rumbling and followed by a giant shaking.

"What is happening?" Liat shouted.

"I don't know." Tzuri clutched her tight to his chest.

Rahab held herself in the window and tried not to fall out into the sand.

Salmon stood right behind Joshua as they listened to the shouts of the people fall silent.

The wall in front of them began to shake and crumble.

"We are coming for you, Rahab," Salmon whispered under his breath.

He raised his sword high in the air.

"Go get the harlot and her family." Joshua turned around to face Salmon and Caleb. "Once they are safely out, we will attack," he shouted over the sound of the wall falling down in front of him.

Salmon and Caleb nodded in unison. They ran up the fallen stones to clear the empty streets toward their target.

Loud banging came from downstairs.

"It's probably looters wanting in to steal anything they can," Liat said.

Rahab left her place at the window. "Let me through," she said, pushing past her family. She rushed down the steps, skipping as many as she dared.

"Rahab!" Alma shouted, following after her.

"I must see," she said over her shoulder. When Rahab reached the door, she heard shouts.

"Rahab!" voices yelled from the other side of the wooden door.

Making her way to the door, she pulled the beam up quickly and tossed it to the side. She opened the large door as Salmon rushed inside.

"We have to go, now!" He pulled her to the side.

Caleb grabbed at the closest woman to him. "Come on, everyone. Follow me."

"Grab whatever you can carry and make sure everyone stays together," Salmon instructed. "You must all run quickly." He waved the line of people out the door. "Follow Caleb, he will show you the way."

"These are the spies I told you of. Go with Caleb," Rahab called after them.

Caleb did not let go of Liat's arm as he dragged her down the street with all the others behind them.

Salmon grabbed Rahab's hand. "We must go."

She nodded and grabbed her shoulder bag. Rahab had to run to keep up with Salmon's significant stride.

"Why aren't we heading for the gates?" Rahab asked, breathless.

"We did not come in the gates," Salmon answered.

She scrunched her forehead at him while they continued running.

"We came over the wall," he laughed.

Just then, Rahab saw the piles of rubble where the strong walls of Jericho once stood. Her family ahead of her was crawling over the fallen stones.

Salmon helped her over the broken pieces and away from the city. He yelled to Joshua, "This is all of them."

Joshua nodded and raised his sword high in the air, then pointed it toward the opening. He began to climb quickly over the stones as the other men of war followed his lead.

Most of the men carried swords, while others carried large torches.

Rahab pulled away from Salmon and stared at the exposed streets. Tears streamed down her flushed cheeks as she watched the flames begin to engulf her city. Screams rose from the fire and Rahab felt her body clench. It was not the first time she had heard the cries of young ones as the flames ate at their flesh. She only hoped it would finally be the last.

"Get her out of here," Joshua's voice called from somewhere in the chaos.

Rahab felt strong hands on her shoulders.

"Come on, we need to get you away from here," Salmon whispered in her ear.

She closed her eyes and allowed her frozen muscles to release into Salmon's hands.

He pulled her backward to his chest.

When she opened her eyes, Rahab saw a massive crowd of beings filling the city streets. Their leader, Michael, led his army over the wall and headed toward the ugly creatures. Rahab watched the slaughter of the fallen ones happen right beside the slaughter of her people at the hands of the Israelites.

Before Salmon pulled her away, Rahab

watched Michael strike a large creature clean through its chest, bringing it to its knees. She gasped when she witnessed Michael strike one last blow to the creature's neck. As the head rolled down the street, Rahab saw the eyes which had haunted her dreams since she was young. She looked back up to see Michael staring at her. She wanted to yell to him. She wanted to thank him. To show him her appreciation. But nothing came.

The giant warrior nodded as if understanding her silent words. He turned and ran deeper into the streets of Jericho.

Salmon led Rahab to a large group of women who stood together far from the fighting. "Here, stay with these women," he said as he turned away.

"Where are you going?" Rahab pulled on his arm.

Salmon turned back. "To fight. God has called me to be a soldier. I will fight for you."

Rahab nodded and let go of his arm.

He rushed over the fallen walls.

Once the screams were silenced and the blood ran thick in the streets, the Israelites cleared out of Jericho. They carried with them only what they had been instructed to take. Everything else had been killed and burned. The entire city lay in smoldering ashes as the Wanderers made their way back to their camp.

Not a single Israelite life had been lost in the battle of Jericho.

The night grew heavy as Rahab and her family made camp in the tents of the Israelites just outside the main camp.

Cheering and celebrating had gone on since before the sun had set, and had continued well after. The people were just beginning to quiet down enough to retreat to their tents to sleep.

Rahab's heart was heavy. Her city still burned with the fire of the Israelite's God. The smoke was so thick in the air that it burned her lungs.

She sat outside a borrowed tent to watch the last flames die down. Her family slept in borrowed tents around hers.

Jericho. The city which only the day before had laughed in the face of its enemies, now lay crumpled in a heap under the sandals of the Israelites.

Faces of friends and relatives flashed in her mind. Women Rahab had come to care for and had taken off the streets now lay among them again, though lifeless and still. She imagined the many statues to all her people's gods and goddesses turned to ash, surely still surrounded by mingled offerings. They had not come to help. Just like Astarte had not come to her aid all those years ago. Rahab knew they wouldn't come. The citizens of Jericho died believing they would.

Rahab heard footsteps behind her and sprang to her feet.

"I didn't mean to startle you," the man's voice soothed.

She relaxed her shoulders, but stood straight.

The man stepped closer so Rahab could see his face in the darkness. "I've come to check on you. To make sure you and your family had everything you needed for the night."

Nodding, Rahab looked down.

"You don't have to be frightened." Salmon stepped forward and reached for her. "You're safe now under the Lord's protection."

Rahab recoiled.

Salmon pulled his arm back and let it fall to his side. "I don't mean anything... That is to say I..."

She nodded her head slowly, but held her lips tight.

"I see. If you do need anything, my tent is just down there." He pointed up the row of tents. "You come let me know."

Rahab nodded quietly and sat back down with her face toward Jericho.

"You know, sometimes destruction is necessary," he said slowly as he looked over the fallen city.

Rahab glared up at him over her shoulder.

"I mean, sometimes God destroys something in our lives to make room for something better or to move us on to something new. In destroying Jericho, maybe God is opening up a new door in your life, Rahab."

She stared up at the man who made her breath shallow. Rahab glanced to the city and then back at him. Letting Salmon's words sink in, Rahab nodded and then turned her back to him.

"Rest well, Rahab. You are safe. That I can promise you."

As he turned to walk away, Rahab spoke, but kept her back to him. "I saw them."

"Saw who?"

"The army."

Salmon smiled. "You saw us coming for you?"

Rahab turned her head over her shoulder with a confused look on her face.

Salmon quickly wiped the smile from his lips.

"No," she said. "The army. The mass of giants who stood in the sands around Jericho's walls. After you and Caleb left my home."

Salmon took a few steps toward her. "What army?"

"I saw them." Rahab looked up into Salmon's searching eyes. "You believe me?"

His eyes darted back and forth. "Angels? You saw angels?"

Rahab tilted her head up a little more. "What are angels?"

Salmon's smile returned. "Angels are messengers from God. He sends them to the earth to be our helpers and protectors, but normally we don't see them."

"Oh." Embarrassed, she looked down at the

sand between her sandals.

"People have seen them. Just not many."

Rahab's head quickly popped up. "So, I did see them. They were not images of my imagination."

"I believe you saw God's army ready to fight on His behalf."

"That's what Gabriel said."

"Gabriel?"

"A man who looked like the ones out in the sand. He stood in my home and told me not to be afraid. He showed me the army and also..." She bit her lower lip and looked away.

"Also, what?" Salmon said as he reached for her shoulder.

Rahab pulled away. "I'm not ready to talk about it yet."

Salmon withdrew his hand. "I understand. You've been through a great deal." He paused. "What else did you see?"

"Gabriel said because I helped you, God would reward me by sparing my life. That's when he showed me the army. Told me that they were there to fight the fallen ones."

"Fallen ones. What are they?"

"The things I don't want to talk about."

"I see." He took a deep breath and looked up at the sparkling sky. "I just want you to know that I will be here when you want to talk."

She glanced up to see him staring up at the starry sky. Rahab turned her attention back to the place where her former city now lay in ruins. She took in a deep breath and let the warmth she had felt with Gabriel rise inside her.

Chapter 20

"And Joshua sent men from Jericho to Ai,...
saying, 'Go up and view the country. And the
men went up and viewed Ai.' "
-JOSHUA 7:2

Early the next morning, Salmon was summoned into Joshua's tent for a meeting with the other army leaders.

"Ai is our next target. I will be sending my best men to seek out the land. Salmon?" Joshua's voice boomed in the tent.

Salmon raised his head and meet Joshua's gaze, "Sir?"

"You and Caleb take two men with you and head toward the west. Make your way to Ai and bring back a report as soon as you can."

Salmon bowed and left the tent.

Caleb followed quickly behind him. "Ready for another mission so soon?"

"That is what Joshua has requested. I will go," Salmon said without turning to face his friend.

"Who knows, maybe you will find another harlot there," Caleb laughed.

Salmon stopped in his tracks and lowered his eyes to meet Caleb's. He leaned in. "Do not speak about Rahab in that way. I am your friend, Caleb, but I kindly ask that you keep your comments to yourself about that family."

"Y-y-you got it." Caleb held up his hands in front of him. "I won't say another word." He rubbed the back of his neck. "I was only joking around, Salmon. You know I don't mean any harm."

Salmon nodded and mounted his waiting horse.

Caleb followed suit and the two waited for the other men to join them before the small group rode toward Ai.

Upon returning that night, the men joined Joshua in his tent.

"What news have you about Ai?" Joshua asked as he stood in the middle of his tent surrounded by the spies.

"Sir, it is a small city," one man spoke.

"Yes, there is no need for a great army such as ours to take it," another echoed.

Caleb cleared his throat to gain the full attention of Joshua before he spoke, "Two or three thousand would be more than enough to take such a small city as Ai. Allow us to go and smite it. You will not be disappointed."

Joshua stroked his curly beard. Eyeing the silent man to his left, Joshua asked Salmon, "What have you to say?"

Salmon thought on what he had witnessed at Ai. "It is true what they say. The city is meager and defenseless against us. Even a portion of our army would easily overthrow it."

Joshua narrowed his eyes, relaxed, and then nodded. "So be it. Gather three thousand men in the morning and we shall march to Ai."

"Forward!" Joshua commanded from atop his horse the following morning.

The men rushed forward, ready to defeat another enemy of God.

"I don't like this," Salmon yelled over to Caleb.

"What are you talking about? We live for this."

"Something doesn't feel right." Salmon looked up to the sky. "Maybe we should fall back some."

Caleb slowed to match the slower pace of his friend. "Are you getting nervous?"

"No. I just have a bad feeling about this whole thing."

"Are you questioning God?"

Salmon shook his head.

"Joshua, then?"

He shrugged as he ran off toward the side. "I do not know what I'm saying just that this doesn't feel like the other times we have marched."

"Come on, Salmon, let's..." Caleb called to his friend, but was interrupted by a massive noise that stopped him in his tracks.

Salmon followed Caleb's gaze toward the city of Ai.

A massive army, like none they had seen in their surveying, came running from the city.

Salmon met eyes with Caleb. "Retreat! Find Joshua!"

Caleb nodded and went running back to find Joshua.

Salmon found Joshua moments before Caleb. "Sir, these men came out of nowhere. We must retreat. Let us call our men out of this place of defeat."

Joshua watched in horror as he began to see the children of God fall at the hands of the army of Ai. Through the chaos and noise, Joshua was able to call out, "Retreat!"

The word spread through the men. "Retreat! Retreat!"

After almost an hour of running in the opposite direction from their target, the Israelites were able to collect themselves in a safe place.

"I need a count of the fallen," Joshua screamed at a solider when Salmon found him again.

"Thirty-six men are unaccounted for, Sir. We

can assume they were killed." The solider was shaking.

Joshua took a step back. "Thirty-six. We have never lost a soul before today." He grabbed his head.

"Yes, Sir. What are your orders?"

Joshua shook his head in disbelief.

"Sir," Salmon stepped forward. "I think it's time to go home."

After a few moments, Joshua nodded. "Of course."

They quietly marched back toward the tent city. The silence carried them through the makeshift streets of tents and waiting people.

"Inform the widows," Joshua ordered. "I'm going before the Lord."

When he came before the golden ark of the covenant, Joshua tore his clothes from his body and fell on his face. "Alas, Lord God," he screamed. "Why have you brought your people across the Jordan to deliver us into the hands of the Amorites to be destroyed? We would have been happy to live on the other side of the Jordan."

Joshua beat the ground with his fists and continued to scream into the sand, "Lord, what shall I say? When Israel has just been forced to turn its back on their enemies. Now, everyone in the land of Canaan is going to hear about this and shall surround us and cut off your name from the earth. Then what will happen to your honor?"

Joshua stopped his speech as he heard God

speak to his heart, "Get up! Why do you lay on your face?" He rose and stood before the ark as God continued, "Israel has sinned and has broken the commandment which I gave to them. For they have taken of the accursed thing and brought it in among their own belongings. That is why the children of Israel could not stand before their enemies and had to turn their backs. I will no longer be with you because you are cursed until you destroy the accursed thing from among you." Joshua nodded and allowed God to continue with instructions, "In the morning you shall gather all the people together according to their tribe. Draw lots till you come to the tribe, the family, the household, and then finally when you come to the man. Upon discovering who took the accursed things, you shall burn him with fire, the man, and all he has because he broke the command I gave you."

Joshua stared open mouthed up at the tent ceiling. Then he looked back down upon the golden angels who encircled the mercy seat on the top of the ark. "Yes, Lord. It shall be done as you have spoken."

In the morning, before the sun rose, Joshua gathered the people together. Upon drawing the lot down the line of people, as the Lord instructed, he came face to face with Achan. Joshua looked deep into the dark eyes of the betrayer and pleaded, "My son, I beg you. Give glory to the Lord God of Israel, and confess unto Him. Tell me now what you have done. Hide it from me no longer."

Achan answered, "Indeed, I have sinned against the Lord God of Israel, and this is what I did. When I saw the spoils of Jericho, I coveted the items and took unto myself a Babylonian garment, two hundred shekels of silver, and a wedge of gold. I buried the things in the sand under my tent."

Joshua turned to two men standing behind him and commanded, "Go now to Achan's tent and see if the witness he has given is true."

The two men bowed and then ran to Achan's tent. They uncovered the items from Jericho and brought them back to Joshua.

He took the items in his hands and glared at Achan. "Go," he shouted without blinking. "Go get all that belongs to Achan and bring it to the valley."

Soldiers went running from the group. They gathered all Achan had and brought it into the valley.

Standing in front of the large crowd of the children of Israel, Joshua spoke, "Why have you troubled us?"

Achan held his tongue. He stared into the face of his wife and children standing in front of all they owned.

"The Lord shall trouble you this day," Joshua spoke as he raised his arm to signal the crowd.

With arms raised, all the children of Israel

threw stones and large boulders down on Achan and all he had.

Chapter 21

*"And Achan answered Joshua, and said, 'Indeed I
have sinned against the LORD God of Israel...' "*
-JOSHUA 7:20

Rahab's heart twisted as she heard women
screaming. Rushing from her tent toward the
noise, she witnessed the crowd throwing stones
down into the valley.

She saw Joshua motion his men to pile logs and
pour oil over the collection of stones.

"Now," Joshua ordered.

The men took their lit torches and tossed them
onto the pile.

Swallowing hard, Rahab turned her back on
the flames. Lifting her eyes, she met the face of
Salmon.

"What are they doing?"

"A man was caught with possessions from
Jericho. He, along with his family and all they
own, are being stoned and burned."

The flames of Jericho rushed into Rahab's
mind and tears formed at the edges of her eyes.

"It's hard to watch," he whispered.

She nodded solemnly while peeking back at the fire.

"It's necessary," Salmon said, as he looked over her head at the valley.

Rahab looked back to Salmon and tilted her head at him. "Your God's anger is great towards His people."

Salmon nodded. "Only for the moment. It will cool now that the sin has been dealt with as He commanded."

Rahab thought for a few moments before speaking, "Was He angry with the people of Jericho for their sins?"

"Yes. The evil was great in your city. God needed to clean out the land which belonged to him before we could live in it," he said, as he looked toward the direction of Jericho.

She took a deep breath before asking, "What did the man do?"

Salmon followed her eyes to the flaming valley. "He stole from Jericho and kept things for himself."

Rahab nodded a few times and then closed her eyes.

"God told us not to take anything except the precious metals for his treasury. Everything else was to be burned. Well, almost everything," he said. He reached for her hand and held it gently in his.

Her eyes popped open. She locked glances with him for only a brief moment before Rahab pulled her hand away.

Salmon bowed in half and left her.

"Ah, Salmon," Joshua called. "Come. Come." He waved to a pile of blankets and motioned for Salmon to join him. "We are going back to Ai. It will be ours this time."

"I see."

"We are taking all the men with us and the Lord has instructed that we burn the city just as we did at Jericho. This time we can take the spoils and cattle for ourselves. I will send the commands to the leaders today. We march at nightfall."

"Yes, Sir. It will be as you have spoken," Salmon said, as he rose to leave.

"Wait, there is one more thing." Joshua waved to the blanket.

Salmon sat. "Sir?"

"We are going to do things a little different this time and I'm going to need your help." Joshua raised his eyebrows.

Under the cover of nightfall, Salmon lead thirty thousand honorable men toward Ai, but they marched around the city and hid behind it.

Just before the sun rose, Joshua led the rest of the army of Israel straight toward Ai.

When the army of Ai came out of the city to fight against the children of Israel, Joshua commanded his soldiers saying, "Fall back."

The entire Israelite army turned their backs and ran from the men of Ai.

Once they were far enough away from the city, Salmon saw Joshua raise his spear high into the air. That was the signal for Salmon's army to charge the city of Ai.

When the men of Ai's army turned around and saw the smoke coming up from their city, the army of Israel turned to fight the men of Ai. Salmon lead the army of Israel out of Ai after they had set fire to everything in the city and ran to help the other part of their army. Not a single person of Ai was left alive, except the king of Ai whom they took to Joshua.

Two men brought the king of Ai toward Joshua as he begged for his life, "Mercy. Mercy. Please, have mercy."

Joshua stared down at the groveling man. "Hang him."

"NOOOO!" the king yelled as he was drug away to the nearest tree.

The soldiers quickly tied a strong rope around his neck and hoisted his body high in the air.

As the breath left his body, the king's screams could be heard for miles until silence filled the air.

Many watched as the body swung in the wind until the sunset.

"Take him down," Joshua commanded.

The nearest soldier climbed the tree and used his knife to sever the rope. The corpse fell in a heap to the ground with a thud.

"Throw it in front of the gates of the city and stone it," Joshua's instructed.

Salmon stood in front of Joshua. "Don't you think you have made your point?"

Joshua squinted his eyes. "I am about to. They will be punished for making fools of us."

"There is no one left to prove anything to. You have killed them all. Let their king's body rest."

Joshua looked past Salmon. "Stone him."

So, the people of Israel picked up stones and threw them on top of the king's body until a large pile formed.

After the last stone was thrown, Joshua ordered, "Let us move on from this place."

When the group got to Mount Ebal, Joshua made an altar to God and also made a copy of the stones of the laws of Moses. When he finished writing, Joshua read the words aloud for all the children of God and the foreigners among them to hear.

Rahab stood behind the group of Israelites listening to Joshua read.

Salmon approached her, but kept his distance. "You seem to be heavy hearted," he wondered aloud without making eye contact. Out of the corner of his eye, he could see her nod. "These laws apply to you and your family now, but you do not have to fear our God." Salmon heard a huff escape Rahab's mouth.

"All I have seen from your God is anger and hatred," she said.

"Not true..."

Rahab turned her body to face Salmon and waited for him to finish.

"He spared you and all your family."

She was silent.

"God is just, Rahab. You would do well to remember that. He has a purpose for everything He does and everything He allows."

She shook her head as she looked down at the sand. "I thought He was different than the bloodthirsty gods of my people."

"Though His methods can be extreme, the lessons are well learned. Watching Achan and his family be killed was hard, but do you think anyone will try to take what does not belong to them without thinking about Achan and reconsider their action?"

"I see the point." She turned back to the mount to listen to Joshua read to the people.

Later that same day, Salmon entered into Joshua's tent.

Caleb was standing with Joshua and several of the army leaders.

"The kings of the other cities are gathering themselves together to make war against us," Caleb said.

Joshua nodded.

"Sir, we must gather to together all the able bodies and prepare for the war at hand," Caleb continued.

Joshua remained silent.

"What are we waiting for?" Caleb blurted.

"The Lord to answer," Joshua said, emphasizing each word.

Caleb stormed out of the tent and many of the leaders followed him.

Joshua sank to the floor and began to meditate.

Salmon walked over to one of the remaining leaders and asked, "What is this meeting about?"

"Caleb is ready for us to go to war with all those who are prepared against us. Joshua wants to wait. He hears silence and does not want to step out of God's plan again," the captain said and then left the tent.

The remaining soldiers followed him.

Salmon watched Joshua for a few moments. When he heard the sound of approaching people, Salmon left the tent to see who was coming toward them.

Caleb and another captain were talking with a group of foreign men.

"Salmon," Caleb called to him. "These men

say they are from far away. They are requesting to lodge with us."

Salmon confronted the men. "Where are you from?"

"Far away. In a land that is desolate with war. We come seeking peace," one of the men said with a dry voice.

"Go get Joshua," Salmon commanded the captain.

Upon his return, the captain introduced the men to Joshua.

"Greetings, honored leader of the Israelite army," one of the men said, bowing to Joshua. "We come seeking refuge in your camp for we have heard of the wonders your God has done for you. We heard how He destroyed the kings of Jericho and others on your behalf and gave you the land to inhabit."

Joshua nodded and looked them up and down.

The man nervously continued, "When the people of our country heard of all your great victories, the elders told us to take gifts and bring them to you, to ask for peace between our groups."

The oldest man pulled out a loaf of bread from his sack. "As you can see we have traveled a long way because the bread we brought for you has become moldy. And these," he pulled a wineskin sack off his belt and stretched it out to Joshua, "they were new the day we left to come to you. See they are torn with age because we have traveled so far."

Another lifted up his foot. "See our shoes and clothes which we wore here are worn from the long journey across the sand to bring you these peace offerings."

Caleb stepped closer to Joshua and leaned to whisper in his ear, "Sir, these men have traveled far and they seek to do us no harm. Shall we make peace with them and their country?"

Joshua looked upon on all the evidence and nodded his head. "Welcome to our group. Please accept peace from us as we accept your gifts to us. Let us go into my tent and we will make a pact between our people. There shall be no war."

Chapter 22

"And when the inhabitants of Gibeon heard what Joshua had done unto Jericho and to Ai, They did work wilily, and went and made as if they had been ambassadors..."
-JOSHUA 9:3-4

Two days passed, as the visitors made themselves comfortable in the camp of the Israelites.

On the third day, Rahab walked through the tents to find some material to make a new garment when she ran into one of the strange men. At first, she did not recognize the man until she passed him. Looking back over her shoulder, she remembered his face.

Rushing to find Salmon, Rahab began to question him about the stranger. "Who was that man? What business does he have here among our people?"

"Slow down, Rahab." Salmon grabbed her shoulders and looked into her eyes. "What are you talking about?"

Rahab pulled against him, trying to bring him to the place where she saw the man. "Him, what is he doing here?"

Salmon followed Rahab's finger to a man who was walking with Joshua.

"The traveler?"

"Traveler?" Rahab shook her head. "From where did he say he came?"

"A land far away. They had worn clothes and brought moldy bread as gifts for a peace offering."

"Peace offering?" Rahab's breath quickened. "They asked for peace?"

"Yes." Salmon pulled Rahab close to him. "Why? What is going on? Why does any of this cause you such concern?"

She pulled in a few deep breaths as she watched Joshua and the traveler disappear into a tent. "He's lying."

"What?" Salmon spun Rahab around to look her in the eyes. "What are you talking about?"

Rahab wondered whether or not she should reveal the man's identity. She figured anyone who sided against Israel's God deserved no such protection. She sighed deeply and hung her head. "I know him," she whispered.

Salmon lifted her chin. "Come with me." He grabbed her hand and led her into his tent. After making her comfortable, he sat down beside her and said, "Now, nice and slow. Tell me what is the matter with this man and how you know him."

Rahab took a deep breath and began, "He is not from far away. He is from Gibeon and he used to be an ambassador for their city. In my trade, I *entertained*," she choked on the word, "a lot of ambassadors and he would always come to me for more. He paid well, so I would not turn him away." She took another deep breath. "He must have lied in order to gain peace so you wouldn't destroy his city like you did Je-J-Jer..."

"I see," Salmon said softly. He was quiet several moments before he spoke, "Thank you for telling me. I need to go to Joshua. We cannot go back on the agreement, but he'll think of something."

Rahab rose to leave.

Salmon grabbed her hand and brushed it against his cheek. "I'm glad to hear you feel welcomed here."

Rahab tilted her head to the side as she stared down at him.

"You said 'among *our* people' when you were worried about the men causing us danger," he said, with a slight smile.

She thought on the past few moments. "I'm sorry. I did not mean to include myself in..."

"Don't." He stood and placed his hand on his chest. "It makes my heart glad that deep down inside you do."

Rahab looked down at her feet as she felt the blood rush to her face. She ran out of the tent.

Salmon watched his tent flap blow in the wind a few times behind Rahab before he made his way to find Joshua.

Caleb was just leaving Joshua's tent when Salmon headed towards it. "Everything alright, Salmon?" Caleb asked as his friend passed by without a word.

"Sir," Salmon bowed to Joshua, "I have information about the men that now dwell among us from afar.

Joshua lifted his head to stare at Salmon. "What is it?"

"They are from Gibeon, not from a far off land. They are our neighbors and they have lied to us."

"What?"

"It's true, Sir, I have it from a very reliable source," Salmon stated.

"Reliable source, eh?" Caleb said as he entered the tent.

"Yes."

Caleb gawked at Salmon, "Who? That harlot of yours?"

"As a matter of fact," Salmon said as he crossed his arms over his broad chest. "Rahab was the one who told me about the lies of the men."

"Did you ever consider that she may be the one who's lying?"

Salmon squinted his eyes at his friend. "She would not lie to me."

"Sure," Caleb huffed.

"Men, enough," Joshua interrupted. "I will deal with this. Bring me the harlot."

Salmon lifted his eyebrows.

"Rahab," Joshua corrected himself.

Moments later, Rahab stood in front of the small group of men in Joshua's tent.

"The truth is all I am after," Joshua assured her.

Rahab kept her eyes toward the dirt. "It is true, Sir. The men are not from a faraway land. They are from Gibeon."

"You know this, how?"

Rahab glanced quickly at Salmon before returning her gaze downward. "One of them was a client for a long time."

"You must have had many clients," Caleb interrupted. "How do you know this is the man?"

"It's true. That which you say, but I know the man. His name is Ahio and he..." the words caught in her throat.

"Take your time," Salmon said.

After a few moments, Rahab looked up to meet Joshua's eyes. "He kidnapped me from the Temple in which I served; paid off the priest. I spent months in his home, being his personal concubine before I escaped. I know his face. I know the man."

"Thank you," Joshua nodded. "Bring me the travelers."

Caleb bowed to Joshua and then left to obey his command.

Before the whole congregation, Rahab and Salmon stood beside Joshua.

The leader questioned the travelers, "Why have you tricked us? Telling us you come from far away and asking for peace."

The men exchanged glances without answering.

Taking their silence as a confession, Joshua continued. "From now on, you are cursed among us. You shall never be free from under us. All of you will be gatherers of wood and water for the entire camp."

One man answered, "It was because we heard how the Lord your God commanded his servant Moses to give you all the land. To destroy all the inhabitants of the land before you. We were afraid for our lives because of you and have done this thing."

"The woman who stands among you," Ahio yelled. "She is a runaway concubine of mine."

Rahab looked to Salmon.

The people's murmurs began to stir.

"This claim is true," Joshua said. "This woman has confessed all to me in the presence of two witnesses."

"She belongs to me," Ahio broke in.

"I belong to no man," Rahab bit back.

"Silence," Joshua commanded. He turned to the group of men. "Now that your people will be servants to us, you cannot legally own slaves. Since you did not make her your wife, you no longer have a claim on her. Our God has also given Rahab and her entire family into our protection for her acts of faith. She belongs to our camp now. She is free."

Rahab looked over to Joshua.

He narrowed his eyes at Ahio, daring him to speak again.

Ahio held his tongue.

One of the older travelers spoke up, "Ignore the man, master. He is crazed. Now, we are in your hands." He stepped toward Joshua and bowed. "What seems right to you, do unto us."

Joshua answered, "You will do as I have said. Go from me. Be servants unto this congregation and unto the altar of the Lord, even today."

Rahab moved to leave with Salmon.

Ahio rushed her and caught her arm. "They can't protect you forever."

Rahab shot him a narrow glance.

"Still as pretty as ever. Even when you are angry," he said, pulling her close.

"Is he troubling you?" Salmon stepped beside her.

Rahab looked down to Ahio's arm grasping her.

Salmon cleared his throat.

Ahio released her.

Rahab kept her eyes on Ahio. "No. He was just leaving to fetch some water."

"Yes," Ahio growled and bowed low. "It shall be as you have commanded."

"You'll do well to remember your place, servant," Salmon grunted.

"Of course, Master," Ahio held the word while he bowed again.

"How does it feel to be the one to have your will bent?" Rahab asked.

Ahio straightened and lifted his nose with a huff. He turned and walked away from them.

Rahab rubbed her arm.

"Tell me truthfully, was he bothering you?"

"No." Rahab shook her head. "I almost feel sorry for him."

Salmon furrowed his brow.

"I may be low in your camp. But at least I'm free. He will never know freedom again."

Weeks passed.

Salmon stood in Joshua's tent when the men of Gibeon interrupted their meeting.

They pleaded, "Protect your servants. Come to us quickly and save us. Help us, for the kings of the Amorites that dwell in the mountains are gathered together against us."

Joshua looked down at the bowing men before him.

"We may be your servants, but you agreed to defend us with our pact of peace," the oldest reminded him.

"Send word," Joshua instructed his leaders. "We are heading to Gibeon to fight against the Amorites,"

Rahab found Salmon as the men were preparing to leave. "Are you going as well?"

Salmon turned around to see Rahab staring at his feet. "Yes. I have to. I'm a man of war."

"Oh," Rahab sighed.

He walked over to her and lifted her chin, kissing her forehead he said, "I will return to you. I promise."

As Salmon turned to leave, Rahab spoke, "Wait."

He turned back to face her.

"There is something I think I'm ready to tell you."

Salmon stepped closer to her and looked deep into her eyes. "Go ahead."

She took a deep breath to steady the rising fear from her past. "Do you recall when I told you about the army?"

Remembering their conversation, Salmon nodded.

"And do you remember that I told you Gabriel told me that the army was there to fight the fallen ones."

Again, Salmon nodded.

"He showed them to me."

"The fallen ones?"

Rahab nodded as tears began to flow down her cheeks.

"Shh..." he soothed and reached to wipe them away.

"They were awful."

He grabbed her and held her close. "Why are you telling me now?"

"When Gabriel showed them to me, it wasn't the first time I had seen them."

Salmon brushed away some stray hair from her face.

"When I was young, I saw them. They hurt me. It changed my life. I was never the same."

"They hurt you?"

She looked up and nodded slowly. She buried her face in his chest.

"Regardless of the past, you are here with me now." He wrapped his arms around her. "You are safe. I've vowed to protect you and your family."

Rahab hugged him tighter.

He pulled her back to arm's length and said, "I will return to you."

Chapter 23

*"Likewise also was not Rahab the harlot justified
by works, when she had received the messengers,
and had sent them out another way?"*
-JAMES 2:25

Salmon followed Joshua along with all the men of
war to Gibeon.

While they were traveling, the Lord spoke to
Joshua saying, "Do not be afraid, I have delivered
them already into your hands and not one of them
will stand before you."

As the army came close to Gibeon, Salmon
heard strange noises. "Caleb, do you hear that?"

Caleb nodded. "I'll ride up ahead," he said,
urging his horse forward.

"Right behind you," Salmon said.

When the two came close to the Amorite
camp, they were amazed. Bodies lay everywhere
around them in a large pool of blood.

Joshua came up behind them. "What
happened here?"

"It looks as if another army got here before we
did," Caleb answered, surveying the massacre

before them.

"Are they all Amorites?" Joshua asked.

"Looks to be so," Salmon replied.

"Let us go and check," Joshua pointed his horse toward the camp.

The Israelites marched through the fallen Amorite soldiers.

"I think I see them," Caleb said ahead of the group.

"After them," Joshua cried.

"It's getting dark, my lord," Salmon said, peering up into the sky. "Perhaps it's a trap."

"Would they slay so many of their own to trap us?" Joshua wondered out loud.

"What is that?" Caleb pointed to the sky.

Salmon turned to look where Caleb pointed. The darkening sky came alive in bright streaks of fire and rocks. He watched as the sky fell in large chunks straight toward what was left of the Amorite army who ran from them.

Joshua motioned for the army to follow him.

"It must be the Lord," Salmon said. "The stones are falling on the fleeing soldiers."

"There must be thousands of men there," Caleb said, with a shake of his head.

Through the night, the Israelite army watched the sky rain down on the Amorites until the sky finally cleared.

When the sun shone bright, Salmon saw the remaining soldiers fill into the nearby valley. "Joshua, those are the last of their army." He pointed to the valley.

Joshua rubbed his beard. "I have an idea."

"Command me, lord," Salmon said with a bow.

"Not you," Joshua smiled as he looked up into the sky.

"My lord?"

Joshua marched up to the highest place he could find. "Sun stand still and Moon stand still in the valley of Ajalon," he shouted.

Salmon looked up to see the sun and moon stand in their place in the clear blue sky.

"March to redeem yourself," Joshua called to the army.

Salmon and Caleb lead the men into the valley.

After the war was over, Joshua called back into the sky, "Return to your order."

"Joshua." Salmon ran to his leader. "Sir, the five kings have hidden themselves away in the cave at Makkedah."

"Put large stones in the mouth of the cave and set guards on it," Joshua commanded. "Then go and finish off anyone who was left behind. Don't let them enter into the cities because God has given them over into our hands."

He fled to deliver the order.

After the army of Israel had killed all their enemies, the group returned to the cave in Makkedah with Joshua.

"Remove the stones," Joshua directed. "Bring out the five kings."

Caleb and Salmon entered the cave and

brought out the kings and made them kneel before Joshua.

"Men of war, come forth to me and place your feet on the necks of these kings."

The leaders of the Israelite army stepped forward and did as Joshua commanded.

"I show you this day," he spoke to the gathering of people, "what the Lord will do to anyone who comes against us. Fear them not."

The crowd cheered before Joshua and the captains.

Joshua reached for his sword and pulled it from his belt. Lifting it high in the air at the continuous cheers from the people, he sliced the necks of the kings who lay under the captains' feet.

Replacing his sword, Joshua ordered, "Hang them."

The captains sharpened five long poles and lifted the bodies of the kings high.

When night fell on the land, Joshua ordered, "Take them down so we do not defile this land. Throw them into the cave in which they had sought refuge."

After the leaders did all he ordered, Joshua had one final command, "Place the stones back over the mouth of the cave so that all will know. Here lie the bodies of their kings."

Joshua and the people of Israel moved from city to city making war with all the inhabitants of the land which the Lord had promised to them.

When the fighting was done, Salmon sought out the father of Rahab. "Sir," he said over a shared meal. "I would like to pay a bride price for your daughter, Rahab."

Tzuri popped his head up and stared at the man before him. "Rahab?"

"Yes, Sir. Your oldest daughter. I would like to pay her bride price."

"She is not for sale as a wife," Tzuri explained. "She sells herself, so anyone can buy her."

"No, Sir. She doesn't sell herself. She has not sold her body in years."

"I will not accept money for a daughter I do not own. Now, if you are interested in a daughter of mine. I do have one I could offer to you for ten pieces of silver. My Alma is still young and could bear you many children."

"No." Salmon pushed down the anger that grew in his chest. "I wish Rahab to be my wife and no other."

"Why do you seek so hard after a used piece of worthless rubble when she so freely gives herself to anyone?" Tzuri barked.

"It is a great shame that you don't know the woman your daughter has become."

"I told you, that woman is not my daughter." Tzuri snorted. Then after a few moments of silence, he tilted his head at Salmon and asked,

"What has she been doing if not selling her body?"

"She works with some of the other women making garments and other things to sell." Salmon smiled to himself. "She is actually pretty good at it."

Tzuri huffed. "A talent found all too late."

"It's never too late; if someone is willing to change."

"So, what makes you interested in her?" Tzuri dipped his bread into some olive oil.

"I love her," Salmon said simply.

Tzuri smiled. "You and every other man who has ever laid eyes on her."

"It's not like that." Salmon put down his bowl. "I haven't been with her. I was one of the spies she hid in Jericho. She saved my life that day and I haven't been able to forget her."

"Take my advice, young man, try harder to forget."

"I won't. I want her to be my wife."

Tzuri looked the younger man up and down before shaking his head. "I'm sorry; she has not been my daughter in a long time. I have no say over her husband and do not wish for such shame on my family."

Salmon left the tent with a heavy heart. He had known speaking with Tzuri was going to be difficult. Though he never thought that a father would refuse an offer for one of his own daughters. Even more so, that a father would disown one of his children so easily. He went to the next person he could think of that could offer a solution.

"Caleb, do you have a moment?" Salmon tucked his head into his old friend's tent.

Caleb nodded and left his family behind to meet Salmon out in the night air. "What's wrong, Salmon?"

"I just went to Tzuri," Salmon said as he took a few steps away.

Caleb followed. "The old man from Jericho?"

"The same. I went there to ask for Rahab's bride price."

"You want her as your wife?" Caleb stopped.

Salmon stopped and turned to face his friend. He nodded sharply.

Caleb smiled. "It does make sense now."

"What?"

"Why you never married any of the other girls." He laughed. "So, how much did you end up paying for the harlot?"

"Nothing."

"Wow, you got a deal. A free wife."

"No, you don't get it. He wouldn't let me have her. He said Rahab is not his daughter. He was not accepting any money for her."

"I'm sorry." Caleb softened. "I know how much you have grown to care for her."

"That's just it. I do care about her."

Caleb started walking again as Salmon followed. "So, what are you going to do?"

"That's why I came to you. I don't know what my options are."

He thought for a moment as they walked. "The only thing I can think of is for you to go to the priests. Maybe they could do some kind of cleansing on her so that she will be suitable for you to marry. Then just pay the priests her bride price and, there you go, you'll have yourself a wife."

"Do you think that will work?"

"Couldn't hurt to ask them. See what they could do."

"Thanks." Salmon placed his hand on his friend's shoulder. "I owe you."

"Go on, get out of here." Caleb punched Salmon in the shoulder. "Go see the priests and get yourself a wife. You don't have too many days left, old man."

Salmon smiled and ran off.

His first stop was the tent of the priests.

"Come in, my son." One of the older men waved to Salmon. "What can we do for one of Joshua's great warriors?"

"If you please, Sir," he said, as he bowed in half. "There is a request that I must ask of you."

"Name it and we will inquire of the Lord whether it be His will," one of the other white-breaded men answered.

"There is a stranger among us that I would like to take as my wife, but she is unclean before us and the Lord. I want to ask that she be allowed to be cleansed so I can take her as my wife."

The priests traded glances before one spoke, "Who is the woman?"

"Rahab. She is the harlot we rescued from Jericho. She hid Caleb and me when we went spying in the land. God used her to bring us a great victory in Jericho and has allowed us to provide protection for her since that day."

"What of her father? Does she not have any family to set a dowry?"

"I have already inquired of her father. He refuses my offers. He claims their family turned her out when she was young and do not count her as one of their own. They make no claim on her and so have no authority to give her away." Salmon waited as the men whispered among themselves.

"Let us ask of the Lord."

Waiting outside for hours, Salmon was finally called back into the tent.

"We have inquired of the Lord and He has answered." The man flattened his long, gray beard. "We are granting your request. Bring the harlot to us tomorrow and we shall cleanse her. Once the ceremony is complete, she will be pure in the sight of our Lord and in our sight. You will be free to take her as your wife."

Salmon bowed deeply. "Thank you, thank you." With that, he left.

Stopping at Rahab's simple tent, he paused. *Would she even want to be married after everything she had been through in her life? What will I do if she doesn't agree?* He took a deep breath and quietly called into her tent, "Rahab?"

Chapter 24

"And Salmon begat Boaz of Rahab..."
-MATTHEW 1:5

Rahab peered out of her tent flap. "Yes?" Seeing Salmon, she softened. "Salmon, please come in." She stepped aside.

"No."

Rahab looked up in surprise.

"I mean, thank you, but I cannot enter into your tent."

"Of course." She stepped out into the moonlight. "Is this better?"

"Yes."

Rahab looked around for a moment and then back at Salmon.

Salmon cleared his throat and concentrated on keeping his knees from giving way under him as he met Rahab's gaze. His voice trembled slightly as he began, "The reason for my visit tonight is to ask a question. That is to say, there is a matter I wish to discuss with you."

She smiled at him. "Go on."

"Right. See, the thing is...I...I've been to see

your father."

"My father? Is he ill?" Rahab stepped in the direction of her father's tent.

"Oh no, please." He motioned for her to stay. "Nothing like that. I went to ask him for your hand in marriage."

"Marriage." Rahab's mouth hung open with the word.

"Yes, marriage."

"But I'm not...not pure enough...and I've already...done so much..." She looked down.

Salmon moved closer to her. "I don't care about any of that." He curled his finger and used it to lift her chin so he could look into her eyes. "I love you."

"You have to ask my father for my bride price," she said, pulling away.

"I did."

Rahab's head popped up.

"He said you were not his daughter, so he could not accept a price for you."

"Oh," she said, glaring back at her feet.

"I've already been to the priests. They have agreed to cleanse you." Salmon lifted her chin again. "You can be pure again. Then they will accept a price for you. If you are willing to be my wife."

"What?" The possibility of cleansing such a filthy body inside and out shook Rahab's inner being. "They can do what?"

"Cleanse you. They have already agreed. It

would be a simple ceremony. Then you will be seen as a clean woman before God and our people. I can take you as my wife."

"They will do that?" Rahab still tried to wrap her thoughts around such an outrageous offer.

"Yes."

"When?"

"So, does that mean you'll do it?"

Rahab looked into his eyes. "Yes, I love you too. Since the first time I saw you, my heart raced inside me. My soul longed to be with yours in a way I never thought possible."

"Tomorrow." He held her close and let out the air he had been holding. "We can go tomorrow."

The following day, Rahab stood before a handful of priests with Salmon beside her.

"Rahab, do you confess your sins and turn from your old life," one of the priests asked.

"I do," Rahab answered as Salmon had instructed.

"And do you ask to be cleansed so that you will be pure in the eyes of God and the congregation of His people."

"I do."

One of the other priests grabbed a bowl. "Step forward."

She turned to Salmon, who helped Rahab take

off her red veil. Rahab stepped closer to the men and bowed her head.

The man poured oil from the bowl over her head. He rubbed the oil into her hair while saying out loud, "Lord, God of heaven and earth. We, Your humble servants, do ask that by this oil, her confession, and our prayers You will cleanse your daughter, Rahab, and make her clean in Your eyes. Forgive her as we forgive her and make her a blessing to Your people."

When the man finished, Rahab looked up.

"Now, Rahab. You are clean before the Lord and are counted as one of His people. Be blessed as you have been a blessing unto us." He leaned over and placed a white veil on her head and then wrapped it loosely about her. "From this day forward, you are clean. Live humbly before our Lord. Go in peace."

Rahab bowed and stepped to the side where a woman was waiting to help her.

She offered Rahab a damp cloth for her face. "The man you came in with will be waiting outside when you are done."

"Thank you," Rahab said, wiping her face.

The woman dipped her head and left.

Rahab rubbed her oily hair between her fingers and lifted some to her nose. The sweet oil relaxed every muscle in her body. *Thank You, Lord of heaven above and earth below.* She adjusted her veil back on her head and stepped out of the tent.

Salmon was there, smiling at her. "Greetings."
She bowed.

"Now that you are a clean woman, Rahab. Will you accept my offer to become my wife?" Salmon asked.

Rahab smiled. "Yes, I will."

Salmon hugged her.

She could hear him inhale deeply.

"I hoped you would agree. I have already made the arrangements with the priests. We can go before them right now. If you're ready?"

She reached out her hand.

After a short blessing from the men in white robes, Salmon took Rahab home to his tent.

She walked around the modest dwelling.

"You know this is only temporary," he said.

She flinched.

"The home, I mean," he quickly explained. "We will live in a real home soon. One made of stone."

Rahab relaxed.

"May I?" he said, lifting his hand toward her head.

She took a deep breath and nodded slowly.

With anxious hands, Salmon reached for her new, white veil.

Rahab instinctively reached to protect it.

He smiled. "Shhh."

Easing her tension, she dropped her hands beside her body and closed her eyes.

Salmon gently unwound the delicate material

from around her head and allowed it to drop to the floor.

She waited with eyes held tightly shut.

He placed his hands on each side of her face and rubbed his thumbs on her cheeks.

Slowly opening her eyes, Rahab looked into the shining topaz eyes of her husband.

He smiled, "Hello there."

She smiled and wrapped her arms around his neck.

Salmon pulled her face in close to his and pressed his lips to hers.

Rahab melted into his kiss and felt her entire body respond to his affection. She pulled her head back slightly and said, "Hello."

Laughing, Salmon wrapped his arms around her waist and lifted her feet off the ground. He spun her around a few times and then carefully laid her on a large stack of skins. He wiped some hair away from her face and looked deep into her honey-colored eyes.

"I don't want you to ever cover these up again," he said as he brushed his finger along her temple to indicate her eyes.

She hesitated a moment before nodding.

"Now," he said, rolling over on top of her. "Let me show you a thing or two."

Rolling her eyes, Rahab grabbed his shoulders and pulled his body close to hers. "We shall see about that," she giggled and kissed him hard.

Several years later, Rahab sat rubbing her large belly on the floor of her stone home.

"It won't be long now," Salmon said.

She smiled and nodded. "Have you thought about names?"

"Of course." He smiled over at her stomach.

Rahab rubbed the top of her stretched out skin and a sadness came over her.

"What's wrong, my beloved?" He came to sit next to his wife as he laid his hand over hers. "Why do you look in such despair?"

"Just a little afraid, I guess."

Salmon tilted his head down to his wife. "Are you worried about the pain?"

"Some, but that's not what is on my mind."

"Then what?"

She sighed. "I know I am older than many women who give birth, but I know God will see me through that part. My fear is that I don't want this baby to become a sacrifice." Rahab looked up shyly into the face of her husband.

"Is that all?"

She nodded.

"Rahab, you will never have to sacrifice our children to the flames of dead gods."

A tear rolled down her cheek. "Promise?"

"I promise." He pulled her in close to his chest.

A scream erupted out of Rahab's mouth.

"What is it." Salmon jumped at the sound. "What's wrong?"

"I think it's time." Rahab grabbed for her stomach and began to grunt at the waves of pain.

"I'll go get the midwife."

Rahab felt each strike of pain waiting for him to return. She knelt on her hands and feet to rock herself back and forth as the woman had shown her.

"Breath, Rahab," the midwife called, entering the house.

"Rahab," another voice called.

"Alma," Rahab struggled. "The baby is coming."

"I'm here to help," Alma comforted. "How is everything progressing?"

The woman above Rahab furrowed her forehead at the interruption. "She is fine," she replied.

Rahab screamed.

"Keep breathing," she whispered to Rahab. "You want to help," the woman turned to Alma. "Help me get her into a different position."

Taking a deep breath and slowly letting it out, Rahab screamed again at the burning pain.

Alma's face was suddenly beside Rahab. "It won't be long now, Sister."

Rahab forced a smile. It only lasted a moment before the pain took over again.

"You can start to push now," the older woman

called.

Rahab felt Alma crawl behind her.

"Lean against me."

Rahab obeyed.

Alma grabbed her shoulders and whispered, "A few good pushes and then you'll be done."

Rahab took in a deep breath, nodded, and bore down hard.

"Good girl. Keep it up."

"You hear that? You are doing it right," Alma comforted. "Try another one."

"A head. A head. The head is out," the woman cheered. "One more big push, Rahab, and your baby will be here.

Inhaling deeply, she bore down hard and pushed.

As the tiny body appeared in the arms of the woman, Rahab let out a scream of relief and collapsed back onto Alma.

She took in a few shallow breaths as the room spun around her.

"Look at your son, Rahab," the woman called to her.

Closing her eyes, she swallowed hard and tilted her head back down.

"He is so beautiful," Alma whispered in her ear.

Rahab heard the baby cry and opened her eyes to behold her son.

The squirmy boy was covered in blood and yelling for his mother.

The midwife cleaned him off as much as she could before handing him to Rahab.

Looking over her shoulder, Rahab saw Alma crying.

"He is so beautiful, Sister," she said, wiping her cheeks on the back of her hands.

Rahab looked back down on the suckling boy. "He is."

The older woman rose and left the room. When she returned, Salmon was behind her.

"You have a strong son," the midwife said, wiping her hands on some clean linen as she went.

Salmon eased across the room to his wife's side and leaned over her to see the face of his son. "What's his name?"

Rahab smiled up at her husband and answered, "Boaz."

Epilogue

"And Naomi had a kinsman of her husband's, a mighty man of wealth, of the family of Elimelech; and his name was Boaz."
-RUTH 2:1

1312 B.C., Bethlehem

The sun shone high in the sky as Boaz straightened his body in the barley field. Pulling out a rag from his belt, he wiped his brow and returned the cloth to its place. Boaz looked out at the large, open land white with crops. His heart swelled with pride at what his hands had accomplished. Not only his hands, but the hands of all of his workers. Seeing the bent over bodies picking in his field gave him a feeling of accomplishment.

The hot weather and long days never chipped at Boaz, but there was a longing inside which pulled him up from his work in that moment.

As his eyes scanned the area, Boaz paused at an odd sight far out in the distance. A stranger was gleaning in his field. It was not unusual to see widows gathering up the dropped pieces, but a young woman caught his attention.

"Jabin," he called his attendant.

A young man hurried over and bowed. "Sir?"

"Go see who that young woman is," Boaz said, as he pointed.

The man bowed and ran off.

Boaz watched as the two talked.

The woman bowed a few times and tried to hand the barley in her arms over to the servant, who pushed it back to her with a few more words.

Jabin bowed to her and then hurried back to Boaz to repeat the message. "She is the Moabite damsel who came back with Naomi out of the country of Moab."

"The Moabite?" Boaz glanced at the servant.

"Yes, sir. I believe she is called Ruth."

"I heard of her story," Boaz said as he returned his gaze back to the woman, who continued to pick up barley that had fallen to the ground. "How long has she been out here today?"

"Since before the sun rose," he answered.

"Go back to her. Tell her she is not to glean from any other field except mine. Tell her to pick with my maidens. She will be safe. Once you have told her, make it known to all the men that they are not to touch her. And one more thing, when she is thirsty, make sure she is given a drink from the water drawn for the workers," Boaz commanded.

The man made his way back to the woman.

After speaking the words to her, he waited for her response.

She placed her hand to her mouth and then spoke to the man, who turned and pointed to Boaz.

Running over to Boaz, the woman fell to the ground and touched her forehead to the earth. "Why have I found grace in your eyes that you should notice me?"

"I heard all about you. How you followed your mother-in-law here from Moab after..." Boaz paused as he looked down at the woman at his feet. "After the death of your husband. You could have stayed in your homeland and gone on with your young life. Yet you chose to be faithful to your mother-in-law. I pray the Lord, God of Israel, repay your faith and give you a full reward."

Ruth looked up at the legs of the man standing above her. "Let me find favor in your sight, my lord. For you have comforted me and have spoken friendly unto your handmaid, though I am not one of your own."

Boaz was quiet for a moment in thought before he answered, "At mealtime I want you to come up to the house and eat with my workers."

"Thank you," Ruth touched her forehead to the ground and then rose to leave his presence.

The young man stood by. "Any further instructions, Sir?"

"Yes." Boaz watched Ruth take her place back in the field. "Tell the men to let her take from the baskets and not to rebuke her. Have them drop some more handfuls of grain on purpose so she can pick them up."

"Yes, sir." The man bowed and ran off to spread the word to all the workers.

<hr />

The following day, after Boaz had shared a meal with his workers and his heart was light, he went to lie down by a row of bundled barley. When the sun rose high in the sky, Boaz stirred at the fear of a presence. "Who's there?"

"I am Ruth, your handmaid. Please place your cloak over me for you are my nearest kin."

Boaz pulled his cloak off the ground and wrapped it around the young woman. "Fear not, young one. I will do as you have requested. The entire city knows you are a virtuous woman. How have you come to this knowledge about me?"

"My mother-in-law, Naomi. When I told her all that you had done for me, she told me of you and instructed me as to what I should do to have you redeem us," Ruth said as she bowed her head.

"It is true. I am your kinsman. Yet there is one who is nearer to you. Stay here tonight and in the morning I will go to him and see if he will redeem you. If he will not, then I will." He brushed her head and patted the ground. "Lie down and sleep."

She did as he requested.

Before the sun rose the following morning, Ruth rose to go out in the field to work.

"Wait," Boaz said.

Ruth stopped and turned toward him.

"Women are not allowed on the harvest floor. Do not tell anyone you spent the night here."

She nodded.

Boaz thought for a moment. "Go get the veil you wore yesterday."

Ruth went to the place she had slept and picked up her veil and held it out to Boaz. He gathered up heaps of barley and put it in her veil.

"Take it and go to your mother-in-law. You do not have to work for your food today."

She bowed and left.

As soon as she departed, Boaz made his way to the city gates. He sat down in a prominent place and waited. It did not take long before Ruth's relative walked by the place where he sat.

"Friend, come sit with me," Boaz called to him.

The man sat down.

Then Boaz called ten of the elders of the city and had them sit with him.

"Naomi, which came out of the country of Moab, sold a parcel of land, which used to belong to our brother, Elimelech." Boaz pointed to his relative. "I am giving you an opportunity to buy it and redeem the land. If you will not, I am next in line to claim the land and will do so if you turn down the offer."

"I will redeem it," the man answered.

"Then when you go to purchase the land from Naomi, you must also buy it from the hand of Ruth who is the wife of the dead. Then you must raise a family with her in the name of our dead family member."

After considering the idea for only a moment, the man answered again, "I cannot redeem the land for myself, lest I mar my own inheritance. I pass the offer to you. Redeem the right yourself."

"You are all witnesses this day," Boaz spoke to the elders. "I have bought all that was Elimelech's. Even more so, Ruth, the Moabite and wife of Mahlon, have I purchased to be my wife to raise up the name of the dead,"

"We are witnesses," the elders spoke in unison.

The leader stood and spoke to Boaz, "The Lord make that which is come into your house to be fruitful and be famous in Bethlehem."

Boaz went back to his home and found Ruth out in the field collecting grain.

"Ruth, come to me," he called.

She ran over to him and bowed.

He raised her face up to his and kissed her. "You are now my wife. This day have I redeemed you and your family's land. You no longer have to pick for your food."

So, Boaz knew his wife Ruth and she bore a son, whom they called Obed. Obed became the father of Jesse, who became the father of David, who became king over all Israel.

Want to find out what happens next?

Bathsheba longed for a child. What she got was a king.

Bathsheba wanted nothing more than to make her warrior husband into a father. She longed to see their features mingled together with fresh life. When he is sent away to fight in another war, Bathsheba is forced to wait even longer. While fulfilling her ceremonial duty, she is stolen away and ravaged by non-other than King David.

She didn't choose to be unfaithful to her husband, but now she is carrying a dark secret. What will happen when her husband finds out? And what will King David do with her when their one-night sin is brought into the light?

Find out in Book 4 of the Faith Finders Series as Bathsheba becomes "A Stolen Wife."

Also by Jenifer Jennings:

Special Collections and Boxed Sets

Biblical Historical stories from the Old Testament to the New, these special boxed editions offer a great way to catch up or to fall in love with Jenifer Jennings' books for the first time.

Faith Finder Series: Books 1-3
Faith Finders Series: Books 4-6
The Rebekah Series: Books 1-3

* * *

Faith Finders Series:

Go deeper into the stories of these familiar faith heroines.

Midwives of Moses
Wilderness Wanderer
Crimson Cord
A Stolen Wife
At His Feet
Lasting Legacy

* * *

The Rebekah Series:

Follow Rebekah on her faith journey through life.

The Stranger
The Journey
The Hope

* * *

Servant Siblings Series:

They were Jesus' siblings,
but they become His followers.

James
Joseph
Assia
Jude
Lydia
Simon
Salome

Find all of these titles at your favorite retailer or at:
jeniferjennings.com/books

Thank You!

My husband: Thank you for your constant love and support.

Shanene: Thanks for being so gentle with the first peeks of this story.

Word Weavers Clay County: Thanks for all your hard work in critiquing my stories.

2016 WW Retreat Critique Group: You guys were amazingly kind to a newbie. Thank you for your grace and wonderful ideas.

About the Author

Jenifer Jennings takes Biblical accounts, weaves in historical research, and adds a dash of fiction to create stories that encourage readers.

She earned a Bachelor's degree in Women's Ministry from Trinity Baptist College and is an active member of Word Weavers International.

Jenifer uses her writing to grow closer to her Lord. Her desire is that, through her work, God would bring others into a deeper relationship with Himself.

Between studying and writing, she is a dedicated wife, loving mother of two children, and lives in North Florida.

If you'd like to keep up with new releases, receive spiritual encouragement, and get your hands on a FREE book, then join Jenifer's Newsletter: jeniferjennings.com/gift

Made in the USA
Middletown, DE
29 November 2022